WITH EVIL INTENT

By Tracy Truesdale

With Evil Intent

For information, address Comfort Publishing, 9450 Moss Plantation Avenue N.W., Suite 204, Concord, NC 28027. The views expressed in this book are not necessarily those of the publisher.

First printing

Book cover design by Colin Kernes

ISBN: 978-1-935361-11-4
Published by Comfort Publishing, LLC
www.comfortpublishing.com

Printed in the United States of America

Acknowledgements

I would like to thank Katie Banaszak for her skillful editing assistance. I appreciate the "Shorewood Reading Club," Janet Mullinax, Cheryl Osborne and Beth Handy for their generous support. I am grateful for the advice and enthusiasm of my brother Jody and my good friend Bill "The Breeze" Brisendine. And finally, my wife Dorenda for keeping me pointed in the right direction.

Tracy Truesdale
January 2009

Dedication

For my sons.

CHAPTER ONE

The raindrops slammed into the windshield as Tom Clark slowed the Buick sedan to pull off interstate 95 into the rest stop. The heavy rain had been falling for the past thirty miles of the trip. But only during the last mile or so had the volume of rain increased to a level that made driving dangerous. The windshield wipers worked as hard as they could but were unable to maintain a clear view of the highway. There were several cars parked in the rest area with other drivers who were probably also waiting for the rain to slacken before continuing on to their respective destinations. There were a couple open spaces near the restrooms. The space Tom chose was next to a large, dark van that he thought would block some of the wind and rain from his car.

Tom was stopping for two reasons. The first was to allow a little time for the downpour to slow. The second was to relieve the pressure that had built up in his bladder since the last stop. He knew that he did not have time to wait out the down pour if he, Rachel and the kids were to reach the beach house in time to have dinner with friends that was planned for the evening.

They were a little late leaving Atlanta that morning. As the girls were getting older, their individual requirements were becoming more complicated. Getting packed for any overnight trip was fraught with seemingly endless discussions over what and what not to take along. The girls were developing strong individual personalities. Audrey, the oldest at twelve, was on the verge of becoming a teenager and her parents were beginning to see the signs of a blossoming desire for more independence.

She was beginning to notice some of the increased freedoms her older friends were enjoying and was looking forward to being able to do some of the things that she saw these friends doing.

At least Melissa was out of the terrible twos and threes, but now at six, she wanted to be more like her older sister. She was becoming pickier about things like clothes and the way she wore her hair. She was beginning to experience peer pressure even in the first grade.

Rachel had to harness all the patience she could during the preparation for this vacation. It took her two full days to get everything packed and ready for this years annual beach outing. When there was only Audrey, she was still a baby, then a toddler and life was much simpler. Rachel was amazed how the number of complications rose with the addition of just one more child. But she did manage to get everything done and they were able to get away at a reasonable time. So far the trip had gone well, that was until the rain began.

These week-long, group vacations began eight years ago. They were looked forward to at first; unfortunately they became a logistical nightmare. Rachel's friends from college and their husbands had become close friends over the years. But with regular additions of new children, and the accompanying individual activities such as soccer, ballet, piano and tennis lessons, the execution of this sacred annual event had developed into a very complicated process.

No one wanted to be the one to suggest that the gathering had become too tedious for fear of insulting or alienating the friendships. Tom and Rachel valued their friends and enjoyed being with them. Recently though, the wives invariably spent too much time discussing every aspect of the harried lives they lived. But none of them had yet to verbalize the stress experienced by all in the planning and execution of this particular event. When that does happen, they may be shocked at how easy a remedy can be developed.

In the meantime, Tom won't rock the boat. He and the other guys decided a long time ago that it would be in their best interest to let the women stumble over a solution on their own.

Tom had considered other options from time to time. Disney World, Universal Studios, the whole Orlando scene is fun but with two little kids now to keep up with, maybe the beach is a more controllable environment. He knew that eventually, something like Orlando will have to be worked in, but hopefully not every year. The girls were still young enough that they had to be watched constantly. And that is easier to do at the beach house. The kids could run and play on the beach and the adults could keep an eye on them from the comfort and shelter of the screened porch.

Tom recalled his childhood and the fact that his family never went on many real vacations. There was an annual visit to the grandparents, and he remembered a trip or two to the mountains, and once to the beach but other that that, he was limited to experiencing life in the neighborhood where he grew up. He had lived on a few acres with a fair amount of woods around that he and his friends played in. As they got older they would camp in the woods overnight. He learned how to hunt small game such as squirrels, rabbit and quail. He learned how to track the quail and flush them at the exact time when he could get a clear shot at them. The long dirt road meandering through the woods later became a favorite nighttime parking place for him and a date. The dark road provided the seclusion for hormone ridden young lovers to learn the secrets of love. In those days cars were large enough to accommodate teenage socializing.

Tom enjoyed his younger days but he wondered what insights he might have been able to gain if he had been able to see more of the world as a young child. The Grand Canyon, the Rocky Mountains, Mexico; his mind wandered. There was a big world out there with many unique things to see and lots of interesting people to meet! That was probably the reason he was willing to take the girls on so many roadtrips. He wanted them to be able to experience the real world sooner than he was able. Besides, he really got a kick out of seeing the wonder of learning new things reflect in his daughter's eyes. Hopefully, when they were grown they would not be overwhelmed by the unknown, or lack the experiences that their peers enjoyed. If possible, he would make certain that Mellisa and Audrey had that head start. He would take them along with him through life, as long as they would stay. Along the way, he would help them recognize the pitfalls and obstacles of living life in today's world. The earlier they learned these lessons the better off they would be, he hoped.

Tom still hadn't come to the conscious realization that the amount of time he and Rachel would actually be with their girls would be short. Time would go by so fast. Sooner than they realized, the girls would be going off to college and the time they would be together would be limited to summers, vacations and holidays.

Later, it would be only vacations and holidays followed by their marriages and Tom and Rachel would be lucky to see them a couple times a year. He planned to make the best of the years he had to spend with his beautiful little girls.

Tom's thoughts were forced aside by the reality of negotiating the rain and the traffic of the rest area. The downpour was blocked slightly by the larger vehicle that was in the parking place next to the one he had chosen. He decided to leave the car running so the heater would stay on. He set the parking brake and glanced back at the girls sleeping in the back seat. They looked so peaceful. Rachel was resting, half-awake on the passenger side.

"Lock the doors when I get out, honey," Tom said. "Do you need to use the restroom?"

"I don't thing so." Rachel said lazily and closed her eyes again.

"O.K." Tom said. "I'll be back in a few minutes." He got out of the car, pulled his jacket up over his head, and trotted-off to the restrooms. Rachel watched him run through the rain and softly laughed at the splashes his feet created. She glanced into the back seat when she heard Melissa yawn and stretch. Rachel knew that Audrey, the oldest at twelve, would be the most hurt if they didn't make it to the beach at least once a year. She had been to all of the past beach gatherings and was getting old enough now to enjoy most beach activities. Six-year-old Melissa was still satisfied with playing in the sand and running from the little waves that chased her up the beach. She enjoyed getting up early, walking on the beach and picking up the seashells that had been washed up by the high tide. Melissa had a rather large collection of shells that she kept on a shelf in her room. Rachel was thankful that Melissa was becoming more self-reliant, no more diapers nor baby food and she was actually in the first grade. They grow so fast, she thought. She loved her girls, but she was glad that she and Tom had agreed that two was quite enough.

Rachel regretted that the annual beach trip had become such a nuisance because she knew how much the girls looked forward to it. She was afraid that if they did not continue the tradition, the relationships with her old friends would fade and her recent revelation that she was aging may become more real than it was now. At thirty-three she was beginning to suspect she and Tom were in a rut. Two careers didn't provide the opportunity for the quality time that the girls needed. She felt that they were forced to depend on teachers and baby-sitters too much to help raise their daughters. But they were careful about whom they allowed to spend time with the girls, considering the world they lived in.

Rachel believed that life was easier for her parents. Her father held the same job his entire working life, a feat difficult to achieve in today's economy. Tom's employment security seemed to be based on quarterly sales results with the potential for his replacement only one or two missed signed contracts away. Rachel's career was a little more stable. As an advertising executive in the firm she had been with since college, she worked her way up to vice president. Tom expected a similar position by now but the computer systems field was going through a rough time and there was not enough room at the top for any advancement.

"The experience is needed where the rubber meets the road," said his sales manager who was only trying to maintain his own position within the company. She and Tom were lucky, though. Several of their friends had gone through downsizing and forced to change jobs just when things seemed to be going well. "You can't take anything for granted these days." She thought to herself.

Rachel considered going to the bathroom, but decided that she could wait. She laid her head back and took advantage of the peace and quiet inside the warm car while the rain attacked the outside in a futile attempt to enter.

The front that was causing the rain made its way up from the Gulf of Mexico and pounded the gulf states for the past two days. It would saturate the southern and coastal areas of South Carolina before finally exiting out into the Atlantic where it would dissipate over colder waters.

Rachel's sleepy thoughts were interrupted by what she thought was Tom returning from the restroom and opening the rear passenger door behind where she was dosing. She maintained her comfortable position, her eyes closed, she tried to go back to sleep. "Maybe Tom is giving the girls a prize from the vending machine or getting something from the back seat floor," she thought lazily. "It has only been a couple of minutes since he left. Has he had time to use the restroom and get back?" Rachel asked herself.

She finally turned toward the back seat, and as she did she briefly caught a blur in her peripheral vision on the left side and felt something go around her face from the back, she slowly faded as she felt a dull thump on the side of her head. Rachel began a scream that died in her throat before it could get out.

Amidst the concealment provided by the rain and darkness that shrouded the rest stop, Tom and Rachel had been observed intently since they pulled into the rain soaked parking space. The observers identified them quickly as carrying cargo which was emotionally valuable to Tom and Rachel Clark, monetarily valuable to the observers. There were no lights on inside the larger vehicle. Tom could not have seen anything to give him suspicion without pressing his nose to the side window because of the heavily tinted windows. He could not see the two sets of eyes peering, with evil intent, in his direction.

The vehicle that occupied the space beside them was a converted full-size van. This particular van was several years old and well past its prime. It was of the condition and age that made it easy to come by at hundreds of small used car lots at a price easily affordable by anyone with enough down payment and the ability to convince the lot owner that cash payments could be made by close of business each Friday.

The men waiting in the darkness of the van had not long to wait. As if right on cue, a promising vehicle pulled into the space on the proper side of the van. The occupants of the larger vehicle were able to see into the Clark's Buick sedan with the help of one of the only operating overhead lights provided by the State Highway Department at the rest area. As soon as Tom disappeared into the restroom, the perpetrators went into action, executing their preplanned actions flawlessly. To a casual observer, it appeared they were simply rearranging things inside Tom Clark's Buick.

* * * * * * *

Tom was thankful for the shelter from the rain when he finally reached the restrooms. He was not thankful, however for the odor that greeted him as he entered. A choking ammonia smell from old dried urine permeated the room. It looked as though the room had not been cleaned in a month. Tom located what appeared to be the cleanest urinal while trying not to breathe more that absolutely necessary. He looked at his watch. Seven-thirty pm, and there was just enough time to get to the island and freshen up for dinner. The group met every year at the Captain's Kitchen, a restaurant typical of the seafood establishments all along the Atlantic coast, except this one provided a little higher level of service.

The usual reservations had been made. They were all expected. The stress of the preparations and travel was nearly over and they would be able to relax at a table of shrimp, scallops or lobster if they felt like splurging. Melissa had developed a taste for crab legs over the years. It was fun to watch her eat them, as she tried to crack the exoskeleton to get to the tender, sweet meat inside. A bib was totally useless during one of these meals. Melissa had a way of pushing it aside a little with every movement. Rachel learned to bring an extra change of clothes for her if crab legs were on the menu.

The evening dinner was the only activity planned for the first day, except, of course for unpacking the vehicles. Tom was thankful as he realized that he would be able to hit the hay shortly after dinner. Following a half day's travel and a generous meal, a good night's sleep was certainly welcome. He hoped to be able to sleep a little later than normal, tomorrow, but he knew the girls would be jumping on him as soon as they got up so that "everybody" could go down to the beach and collect seashells. He'd get up and do his fatherly duties, regardless of how comfortable the bed was. The first morning of the vacation was always the laziest for everyone, except the children, trying to recover from the driving of the previous day and the deep-fried dinner of the prior evening.

After relieving himself and scanning the graffiti on the wall, Tom zipped his pants, washed and dried his hands. He laughed as he realized that drying anything in the midst of the current downpour was a waste of time. He opened the restroom door and while thankful for being able to escape the steaming odors of the restroom, he was apathetic about having to step back into the rain. He pulled his jacket over his head again and hastily retraced his steps back to the car.

As he approached the car he began to see what appeared to be a dark shape on the ground at the left side of his car. Tom wiped the rain from his eyes with his sleeve. A step closer and he could see the shape move, slowly, toward him. It seemed to be trying to raise itself from the ground. Tom took a step closer, the shape rose higher, a step closer, and Tom recognized the nearly unidentifiable shape as a rain-soaked person. "Melissa?" he thought, as he squinted his eyes for clearer vision. A step closer. "Blood, was that blood on her face?" Tom ran the last few steps and grabbed Melissa around the shoulders.

"Mommy, Audrey." Melissa mumbled. Tom shielded her from the rain and looked into the car, he could barely see inside because of the rain in his eyes. The door was open, so he helped Melissa sit down. He looked over for Audrey, but the seat was empty and her door was open. Rachel was slumped over the center armrest in the front seat.

"What the hell happened? I was only gone a minute." He half yelled to Rachel as he shut Melissa's door. Tom ran to the passenger side of the car, expecting to see Audrey on the ground as he had found Melissa, but she was not there. Tom reached for Rachel's door and opened it.

"What happened, Rachel?" He asked his wife in a terrified tone but she did not respond. He saw that Rachel was still slumped over the armrest. He reached in the car and grabbed her by the shoulders and pulled her up. "Was she asleep or unconscious?" he asked himself. Tom gently shook her. "Rachel wake up." He said into her face. "What the hell happened?"

Unsure of what to do, he finally took Rachel's wrist and felt for a pulse. He didn't really know how, but he finally found the small pulsating artery hidden between her tendons. She was alive. He looked back at Melissa, and noticed that she was bleeding badly from her nose and her left eye was gradually swelling and turning a deep purplish blue. She had been crying softly and staring into space as if in some form of semiconscious state. Tom realized that she was softly saying something. He stopped and listened.

"Audrey……, Daddy……, Audrey's gone, Audrey's gone." Melissa cried the words softly through her tears. Tom suddenly noticed that the van he had parked beside was gone. A pang of intense fear shot through him as he digested what Melissa was saying. Tom looked over to where his oldest daughter had been sleeping peacefully just a few moments before. He looked up and into the parking lot. Everything seemed to close in around him. He stepped away from the door and walked to the rear of the car. Then he turned and walked to the front, looking for his oldest daughter. The rain fell all around him.

"Audrey," he said. "Audrey!" a little louder that time. No answer came. He looked around to see if there was anyone who may have seen what happened. There was no one to talk to. He began to feel a scream build in his gut, but he choked it back. His mind was now numb, but he suddenly realized he needed help. There were not many cars in the parking spaces near his car. He ran to the nearest one and banged on the window. The driver of the car was asleep and woke with a start. Tom realized the man was asleep and probably didn't see anything. Tom persisted, talking to the man through the closed window. The man conceded and slowly rolled down his window. "Did you see anyone take my daughter, please?" Tom pleaded and pointed in the direction of his car.

"No, man, I've been asleep." The man responded, concerned but obviously in need of sleep. Tom stared into the man's eyes and concluded that the man had not seen anything and was no help to him. Tom stood and took a couple of steps back toward his car.

"Think." Tom said to himself. He glanced at the building that housed the restroom he had just used. Hanging there on the wall was a round sign. The word on the sign shocked him back to reality a little. He moved quickly back to his car and reached in the front seat over Rachel's semi-conscious body and took the cell phone out of the cup holder. He dialed 911. As the phone rang in his ear he looked at where the van had been parked. It was gone now, gone, possibly with someone precious who belonged here with him.

CHAPTER TWO

With the exception of a few more accidents than normal, caused by the heavy rain over the past several hours, it had been a relatively quiet day at the Colleton County Sheriff's Department. Deputy Rosalee Lingard had just begun her shift as dispatcher when the call came in from the state highway patrol referring a possible kidnapping to the sheriff's department for investigation. Deputy Lingard dispatched the closest unit to the rest area on I-95 just north of the town of Hendersonville, South Carolina where the possible crime took place. Sheriff Deputies Andy Peckham and Vernon Pauley were a few miles south of the rest area at the Steak and Eggs in Jonesville, South Carolina.

The two men were just beginning their first of several food breaks that seemed to occur out of nowhere during their patrol shifts. It gets a little boring cruising the lightly populated area the two deputies are responsible for. They tended to break up the monotony by frequenting the several restaurants they passed on their patrols. A plate of country ham and eggs over-easy and grits with redeye gravy had just hit the counter in front of Andy Peckham when his beeper went off summoning a return call to the dispatcher.

"Shit," Andy said as he reached under his ample waist to search for the beeper. This exercise caused several unnatural contortions of the overweight deputy's upper torso.

"You need to take up joggin' or sumpum, Andy, if you can't even get to that beeper sittin' down," mumbled the middle-aged waitress who served them the same thing every evening about this time.

"Shut up Joyce," Andy growled, "I can get to my beeper. It's my wife's fault for puttin' these pants in the dryer for so long, that's the problem. If I've told'er once, I've told her a thousand times not to do that. I'm forever havin' to buy new pants 'cause of that damn woman and her clothes dryer. Hang'em up and let'em dry I tell'er, but no, she's got to watch TV and talk on the phone." Andy finally retrieved the beeper and looked at the numbers displayed on the little screen.

"Are you going to call or you wont me too?" asked Vernon Pauley, the younger and thinner of the two deputies. Vernon had become accustomed to Andy's diversions from the business at hand and regularly attempted to refocus his partner, at the expense of being on the receiving end of a flurry of verbal abuse.

"I'll call, just hold on to yer horses, it's probably just another wreck anyway, the medics'll be 20 minutes getting' there," mumbled Andy. His years in the Army are revealed by his use of the term "medic" instead of the more civilian "EMT." Ten years as an Army MP had given him the qualifications to be employed by almost any law enforcement agency in the country. His only limitation was an inadequate vocabulary delivered in his southern drawl. After the Army, his search for work did not take him outside of his home state of South Carolina. He had chosen the lowcountry of South Carolina because that was where he and his wife had grown up. He had visited larger cities but felt uncomfortable while there and so did his wife. They were perfectly happy to come back home.

Andy stood, took a gulp of coffee, put his plastic covered trooper hat on and headed out to the patrol car. Pauley correctly predicted that they were not going to have enough time to eat sitting at the restaurant. So he asked Joyce to turn Andy's ham and eggs into a sandwich while he gulped his down. After choking down his food, Vernon grabbed Andy's sandwich, paid the check and headed out to the cruiser where he found his partner talking on the radio. As the dispatcher explained the situation to Peckham, his demeanor changed to one of concern. Pauley knew from the look on his partner's face it was time to go to work.

After Deputy Lingard dispatched the two deputies to the scene, she transmitted a preliminary report to the South Carolina State Law Enforcement Division, known as SLED. This was done so that SLED would be prepared to assist in the investigation if the case was actually a kidnapping, and not simply a lost kid who turned up after following a kitten into the woods. The missing persons division at SLED also prepared a preliminary advisory and forwarded it to the FBI in case their support became necessary. All of these precautions were automatic and occurred every time an initial report of possible kidnapping reached the offices of these state agencies. Nine times out of ten, the missing person was found and further action was not necessary. But the tenth time was not so lucky. All of the efforts of many concerned people from small local police departments through state law enforcement agencies up to the FBI and all of its resources may not be enough. For whatever reason, people can disappear without a trace, are never to be heard from again. In the case of missing children, the primary cause was abduction by an estranged parent who lost custody in a divorce. Although illegal and difficult on the custodial parent, the child normally came to little harm because the non-custodial parent usually loved the child also. It was the taking of an individual by a stranger for reasons known only to the kidnapper that created the most fear and concern among rational people.

The world is a huge place populated with billions of people, each with their own motivations and desires. Human intentions can be good or they can be evil and the entire gamut is reflected in the souls of the populace of this planet. Sometimes it seems that evil is winning; sometimes good, but be assured both do exist and they are actively pursuing their particular aims. Good is naturally passive and trusting whereas evil will do what is necessary to accomplish its ugly goals. Good is at the mercy of evil until it becomes aware and is willing to target the evil force for exposure and hopefully elimination.

Honorable people are constantly at the mercy of the shells and arrows of deceit, fraud, and thievery by the agents of evil. The essence of an effort to control the effects of this activity has to be specific in order to be effective. General efforts at negotiation or outright pleading will only provide one with wicked intent the time and cover needed to carry out its plan. Some recognize this to be true and are providing the means to carry out effective counter campaigns. Persistence is required in such an effort because as soon as one agent of evil is vanquished another will rise from the slime to take its place.

* * * * * * *

Andy Peckham put the cruiser in reverse as Vernon was settling into the passenger seat. Vernon Pauley reached for the door to close it as the vehicle began to move.

"Hold on man, I'm not in yet." Vernon complained.

"Shut the door." Andy mumbled. He backed the cruiser out of the parking place and then headed out onto the small two lane highway. It was one mile to the interstate and then five miles to the rest area. Peckham should be able to cover the distance in about seven minutes. Neither of the two deputies had handled a kidnapping before. All they remembered from their law enforcement training was to question the witnesses, take thorough notes, secure the scene and wait for a supervisor.

"I got your ham and egg sandwich." Vernon said, as he held out the bag of food, he smiled inwardly knowing he'd get no thanks from his grumpy partner.

"Good," mumbled Andy. "Call in and ask if Captain Wilson is going to meet us at the scene."

"Alright." Vernon said as he laid down the bag with the sandwich and grabbed the microphone. "Rosalee, this is Bravo two one, over." Vernon spoke into the microphone.

"Bravo two one, go ahead, over. " Replied Rosalee.

"Is the shift commander enroute to our location, over?" Vernon asked.

"Don't believe so, over." Rosalee Answered.

"Base, I believe shift commander is required on this scene, over."

Vernon said.

"Bravo two one, I'll call him, you're probably correct, over." Replied Rosalee.

"Thanks, out." Vernon said finally. He replace the microphone in its clip on the dash and the two officers drove the few remaining miles in silence.

A few minutes later they pulled into the rest stop identified by the dispatcher. Andy Peckham flipped on the blue lights as he noticed a man get out of a Buick sedan and began waving his arms. Peckham pulled up and parked facing the back corner of the vehicle. Andy Peckham might have been a fat slob but when it came to proper procedure, he had a pretty good memory, especially since most procedures are written to protect the deputy's ass. Tom and Rachel Clark immediately moved towards and began to verbally assault Andy and Vernon as soon as they got out of the cruiser. Tom and Rachel assumed Andy was the senior officer so he was the focus of their verbal attack. Reflex caused Andy to turn his holstered weapon away from the Clarks and ordered them to stand back. The Clarks halted in mid-step briefly, and then continued approaching.

"What the hell took so long?" screamed Tom. "Where are the others? You need more that one car to search the area around here. Where are the others?"

"Just relax sir, our supervisor is on his way. Now settle down, please." Andy said. The man standing in front of him was extremely agitated, almost hysterical. Tom was soaked and obviously terrified. Andy instinctively kept his hand at the butt of his service revolver, although he had the feeling that these people had indeed met with some sort of personal disaster. The rain soaked man seemed to ignore his words and continued his pleading.

"My daughter has been kidnapped, get on your radio and get more people here, we have to look for her!" yelled Tom. Rachel was crying and holding on to Tom's arm. She was soaking wet also. Vernon noticed that the woman appeared to be on the verge of a nervous breakdown. In addition she had sustained an injury to her head. Sobbing uncontrollably, she glanced quickly and nervously between the two officers as if mentally pleading for them to help.

Vernon Pauley stepped around the passenger door of the cruiser and approached the couple. As he did he noticed the small passenger in the backseat of the Buick. He stepped to the side of the car and looked in to see a wet, crying and bleeding little girl.

"Hello, are you O.K.?" asked Pauley looking the girl over, taking note of her injuries.

"Yes sir, but my head hurts a little and where's my mommy?" the little girl asked.

"She's outside, she'll be back in a minute. You just sit tight, O.K." Pauley said, trying to reassure the little girl. He smiled again, turned and approached the three others at the rear of the car.

"Sir, we are going to try to help but we have to ask you some questions, O.K?" Pauley said, attempting to interrupt the man who was screaming at his partner. Tom Clark looked over at Pauley as if he did not realize that he was standing there. The younger deputy stepped closer and asked them to follow him over to the shelter. The Clarks followed the deputy to the shelter while Andy walked back to the cruiser to get his flashlight. While Vernon Pauley questioned the couple, Peckham examined the area around the Buick. The rain, which seemed to have lightened a little over the past few minutes, would certainly have washed away most evidence. But Peckham would rather pursue a seemingly futile search than have to deal with the emotions of the two people with his partner.

"Start at the beginning and tell me what happened." Pauley instructed the rain soaked couple.

"O.K., O.K.," Tom said attempting to regain his composure while holding a sobbing Rachel around her shoulders. He was breathing hard and could barely speak. "I pulled in and parked. I went to the restroom. While I was inside, someone took her, they took her." Tom said, on the verge of tears, barely able to control his emotions.

"Did you see who took her?" asked Pauley.

"We don't know, they hit my wife and my other daughter and they were unconscious when I found them, they did not see them, we have to look for her," cried Tom shaking his head, his body was now trembling involuntarily. Rachel was still holding onto his arm as if she couldn't stand on her own.

"O.K., please relax sir, we have more help on the way." Pauley said "I need you to help me get some information, so please calm down." The deputy's attempts to get the people to relax were not working very well. Their current emotional state was beyond his ability to control.

"We didn't see anything. My wife was asleep in the car when it happened," said Tom.

Vernon Pauley continued questioning the Clarks while Andy Peckham searched the parking area. Finding nothing, he retraced his steps to the Buick where he finally noticed the little girl inside. He shined his flashlight inside and estimated her age to be five or six. Peckham opened the rear door of the car.

"Hello, my name is Andy. What is your name?" he said to the little girl.

"Melissa," she said softly. Peckham noticed her injuries.

"What happened to your face, Melissa?" Peckham asked.

"A man hit me," she said. Andy realized that she might be the only person that may have seen anything that could help find her sister.

"Did you see the man?" he asked carefully hoping not to upset her.

"I saw him get out of the truck. He opened my door. But, then he hit me and I don't remember anything after that." Melissa said softly. Peckham was checking the wound on her face when a reflection flickered in the cars window. Peckham looked up as a set of headlights illuminated him from the rear. Another cruiser was pulling up. A uniformed officer got out of the vehicle and approached Peckham. It was the state highway patrolman for the area, PFC Mike Long of Walterboro, South Carolina. His assigned patrol covers I-95 from Walterboro south to the Georgia state line.

"Melissa, I'll be back in a minute, O.K." Andy said. "See if you can remember what the man looked like, can you do that for me?" She nodded her head and he softly shut the car door. "Hello, Mike." Andy said as the patrolman approached.

"Is there anything I can do to help?" Long asked. Andy explained to the patrolman what they had learned so far. He mentioned to the patrolman that the little girl said that she saw a man get out of a truck.

"Sounds like their other daughter has been abducted but we don't really know what to look for," Peckham said. "The parents didn't see anything, not a face, not even the truck that the little girl saw."

"The woman appears to be injured. What does she remember?" asked Long.

"Nothing, she was strangled and struck in the head and maybe chloroformed. She was out at the beginning." answered Peckham. "My partner may have gotten more information by now. We'll talk to him in a few minutes."

Vernon Pauley was still questioning the Clarks when Captain Wilson finally pulled up and got out of his cruiser. Captain Stan Wilson, and eight year veteran of the Walterboro sheriff's department was a good cop. At forty-five years old, he was in top physical condition. About six feet tall, his short cropped black hair framed a square face and he presented a professional demeanor. His men respected him. They knew they could count on him to be fair, even if a decision didn't go their way. After graduation from the Citadel in Charleston with a degree in criminal justice, he accepted a commission with the United States Air Force. He and his new wife looked forward to seeing the world. They had both grown up in Charleston and they planned to return to the lowcountry after his career in the Air Force was completed.

Wilson spent twenty-three years in Air Force blue in law enforcement. He commanded security police units at several bases stateside and did four stints in West Germany prior to the wall coming down. His last overseas tour was in Iraq in nineteen ninety-one where he commanded a security police company guarding the airbase at Riyadh, Saudi Arabia. A skirmish on the base perimeter had provided sufficient cause for the

Air Force brass to bestow him a Silver Star.

Peckham briefed Wilson on what they had learned so far, especially the information obtained from the little girl. Captain Wilson along with Peckham and Long walked to the shelter where Deputy Pauley introduced Wilson and Long to the Clarks. After handshakes, Wilson suggested that the Clarks follow him to the sheriff's department headquarters while the patrolmen begin their search. Tom and Rachel seemed to calm down a little with the knowledge that a search was actually beginning. Mike Long returned to his cruiser and radioed his dispatcher to request additional patrolmen to assist in the search, even though they had no idea what to look for, except for the vague reference to a truck made by the little girl. Tom and Rachel Clark returned to their car and prepared to follow the officer to the sheriff's department.

As Captain Wilson was leaving the rest area with the Clarks in tow, he notified the dispatcher to alert all units of the abduction and for all units to be on the lookout for anything unusual. He also instructed Lingard to contact all adjacent counties and notify each department of the need for assistance in the search. Wilson provided her with a description of the girl and the fact that they may be looking for some kind of truck.

The call from the dispatcher went out to the surrounding counties shortly after a car was pulled from the ditch along a lonely road in Beaufort County in the midst of a torrential downpour.

CHAPTER 3

The weather had provided the cover and concealment needed, and the complacency of the victim's parents had provided the opportunity. Only a few minutes of waiting for the correct set of circumstances to unfold was necessary and when it did, the perpetrators took advantage of it. The action had been carried out with the efficiency of a practiced military operation. With the little girl extracted from the car and immobilized, they were on their way in less than one minute. The prize secured, they proceeded to the prearranged location where the transfer would take place. Shortly after exiting the rest area the driver was able to leave the interstate highway and take advantage of the anonymity provided by a dark two-lane road. The van made its way through the rain and wind toward a small marina near Beaufort, South Carolina. The trip, which would normally take about an hour, would be stretched to probably two, due to the weather.

The two men in the front of the van were locals. They were born in the Lowcountry of South Carolina. Lowcountry is a term used by generations of South Carolinians, it describes the coastal area of South Carolina from Georgetown south to the Georgia border. The Lowcountry includes the "Great State" of Charleston, as the inhabitants prefer to call it, due to their belief that Charleston would be a better place to live if the less important balance of the state of South Carolina didn't exist. Blue Blood runs deep back through the centuries in Charleston. The social structure that was established during antebellum prosperity was not far below the surface. The Dixie flag is a constant reminder of where you were. The war was a glorious attempt to maintain the status quo while new ideas about the way people should treat others began to occupy the minds of great thinkers.

The big van had been purchased, inspected and repaired in accordance with the instructions provided by their contact. The success of their mission could easily be compromised by a burned out brake light or a set of balding tires. The vehicle had been purchased with this type of use in mind. And even with it's age, it was in excellent condition. The operators of the van had followed the directions provided by their employer to the letter. The amount of money at stake provoked a sense of seriousness the two had not known in years. This was only the third job they had done for this man. The first two went well and every arrangement had worked out as expected. They had been paid when promised. The two men decided to ride this horse as far as it would take them. The man who had hired them would continue to pay them substantial amounts of money if the missions they were assigned were accomplished according to his instructions. The two also understood that there was a significant price to pay if things went wrong. A southern prison is no place to spend any length of time if one has harmed a child.

The two lowcountry men, Jack Brooks and Tony Means, have never met their employer. He called Jack at home to make any arrangements. Jack was an ex-con and lived alone. At forty-six, he had never held a real job longer than six months. Since a normal life did not seem to suit him, he was forced at an early age to resort to robbery and drugs for his livelihood. He had spent half of his life behind bars. The first time he went up was for rape, at age eighteen. She was twelve.

Tony was a lucky loser. Even though he had robbed several convenience stores and one Waffle House, he had never been caught. He seemed to be a little quicker than those who chased him through the dark woodlands of the Lowcountry of South Carolina. His only setback came during his last convenience store robbery when, while fleeing, he collected several double-aught buckshot in his back, hip and right leg, a painful lesson that prompted the decision to begin robbing Waffle

Houses, a restaurant chain that he has frequented over the years and never noticed a shotgun under the counter. He walks with a slight limp, due to the fact that the buckshot wounds were allowed to heal by themselves with the shot still lodged in his body.

Jack is the boss, not only due to age but also because of his time in prison. Professional criminals view prison as a finishing school and a badge of honor. If they survive until their time is up, they can leave and return to society with a unique and thorough criminal education. Jack was just mean and smart enough to successfully complete his "education" and make some important contacts while in "school." His current employment is the result of the networking skills learned in prison.

Jack and Tony met one night as Tony was stumbling across the parking lot outside a local bar after being on the receiving end of an ass-kicking over a pool game and a glance at the wrong woman. The girl knew how insanely jealous her boyfriend got when other men talked to her. Only she knew the danger inherent in the playfulness between herself and Tony. The flirting did not last long. Tony was caught from the back and never saw the cue stick coming. Tony took several savage blows and was physically ejected from the building. Jack was pulling into the lot and nearly ran over the fool. Tony could not see where he was going due to drunkenness and the blood that had collected in his eyes from the two-inch gash in his forehead. He fell across the hood of Jack's car and off the other side leaving a trail of blood and vomit. Jack, in a rare case of compassion collected Tony and let him sleep it off in his garage that night. He also wanted Tony to be available to clean the hood of his car when he got his strength back. Since then Tony has followed Jack around like a stray cur.

Jack Brooks was a quiet serious man of medium build and a tight, muscular frame. He face is lined with a few wrinkles and one scar on his right cheek from a knife fight while in prison. His jeans were clean and fit, well; the dark grey t-shirt he wore covered the tattoo of a dagger with a snake curled around it on his upper left arm. Jack's family was close when he was young and his parents tried to raise him right but he was not inclined to live the way they had tried to raise him. His brother and sister had gone on to live happy middle class lives. His parents were both dead now and he did not see his siblings at all. Jack was a typical sociopath. He was not able to function in a civil society. He generally did not like people and regarded most people as stupid or delusional in their beliefs. He preferred to be alone. Crowds of people raise an emotional fire in his soul. He likened most of the people he encountered as mere cattle being herded off to slaughter.

Tony Means was not quite smart enough to entertain the deeper thoughts of his partner. A little taller than Jack but slimmer, he didn't care about his appearance and would wear the same clothes for days. His face was somewhat boyish and his hair usually appeared dirty. Tony's father was an alcoholic who was abusive to Tony and his mother. Tony was allowed to run the streets as a young boy and was never taught to develop self-discipline or to strive for accomplishment. He dropped out of high school in the tenth grade. Those who knew Tony were unable to take him seriously. Besides being uneducated, he tended to behave frivolously. He was currently residing in Jack's spare bedroom which he managed to keep as cluttered as he possibly could. Jack would ridicule him for the condition of the room but his words fell on deaf ears. Tony was a slob and there seemed to be nothing Jack could do about it.

Tonight, the two had learned a few new techniques that they would be able to put to use later. The idea to target the rest area had not been theirs. It was a suggestion received along with the assignment. But now they were running late. They sat in the same reststop the two previous nights but had no luck. They were scheduled to make the delivery at the marina tonight. Tony glanced back into the rear of the van. He saw nothing unusual; which was good, he thought. The cargo was tied, gagged and covered with a tarp and lying snuggled between the back door and the rear bench seat.

"Everything O.K. back there?" Jack asks.

"Looks good from here," Tony replied. "How much longer do ya think?"

"Don't know. We'll get there when we get there." Jack said as he pulled a pack of cigarettes out of his jacket pocket and extracted one with his lips. He offered the pack to Tony who took one for himself. Jack had considered firing up a joint but he decided to follow the rule of no drugs or alcohol "while on the clock." His employer had an uncanny way of knowing his personal habits.

"We going to the same boat?" Tony asked as he lit his smoke.

"All I have is the marina and the slip number. Don't know what boat will be there." Jack answered, using a lungful of smoke to vibrate his vocal chords.

The heavy rain caused Jack to pay more attention to driving. Tonight was not the night to have an accident or be pulled over by local law enforcement. Jack was thankful that he had replaced the windshield wipers when he bought the truck. They rode on in silence for a while until they heard a bump from the rear of the van. Jack looked back through the rearview mirror.

"How 'bout you go back there and make sure she is still tied up." Jack said.

"Alright, just a minute." Tony said as he placed his cigarette in the ashtray. As Tony turned and stepped between the seats, Jack rounded a sharp bend in the narrow, wet road and was immediately blinded by the sting of flashing blue lights. Jack slowed quickly throwing an already unbalanced Tony forward against the engine cover, his head hit the rearview mirror and snapped the mirror off its mount.

"Dammit," Tony said as he struggled back to his seat. "What the hell are you doing?"

"Cops, shut up." Jack snarled. About one hundred yards in front of the van was what appeared to be a car in the ditch on the right side of the road. A sheriff's cruiser and a wrecker were there to assist. Jack slowed further and fingered the stolen nine-millimeter automatic that was secured under his left arm. Tony stiffened in his seat. The van approached the scene carefully. Jack noticed one deputy in the road directing what little traffic there was while the wrecker driver hooked up to the car in the ditch. The lights were on inside the deputy's car and it appeared the passengers of the car were inside and the driver was probably being given a ticket. Jack slowed to a crawl as he approached the scene. Tony nervously looked straight ahead and was silent. Jack was concerned that Tony was not acting natural and might tip off the cop if he did not rubberneck like the rest of the rednecks around there.

"Relax, Tony. We'll be alright." Jack said, scared as hell himself but he concealed it well. As the van approached, the cop in the road began to wave his hand to send them around.

Jimmy Harmon was young, just six months with the Beaufort County sheriff's department. He graduated from Beaufort High School the year before and was happy to have finally found a fulltime job. He wanted to ask his girlfriend Donna to marry him but he knew that he had to have a career first. He wasn't sure about joining the sheriff's department, but his dad had been in law enforcement so he understood the lay of the land and has been able to fit in well. He was beginning to enjoy this job now, though training had been tough. He was lucky to be assigned to a partner like Jason Watson. Watson had been with the department eight years and enjoyed training new recruits. He didn't abuse the "newbees" as some of the old timers did. Jason remembered being in their shoes and he didn't appreciate it when he was treated that way.

Unfortunately, this call happened to be a motor vehicle accident and it was raining. Jimmy didn't mind directing traffic in the rain as long as the rain gear maintained it waterproof qualities. So far the only car to come along while he'd been standing behind the cruiser was approaching now. Jimmy saw the approaching headlights reflected against the wet pine trees on the outside bend of the road while the vehicle was still a good ways up the road. When it did finally round the bend, Jimmy was expecting it. He noticed that the driver reacted the same way all drivers do when they come upon blue lights unexpectedly. He watched as the headlights dipped when the driver hit the brakes. He still thought that was funny.

As the vehicle approached, Jimmy dropped the bill of his hat to shield his eyes from the high beams. Startled drivers usually forget to dim their lights. Jimmy checked the other lane and determined that it was safe to send the vehicle around. He began to wave the vehicle through. As it slowed and veered into the other lane, Jimmy recognized that it was an older full-size van. As it went by he noticed that the passenger was a male and he was staring straight ahead as if the other vehicles weren't even there. He was accustomed to everyone wanting to see what was happening, but this guy seemed to be ignoring the activity on the side of the road. Jimmy watched the van go by and noticed that all of the lights were working and the license plate was lighted as it should have been, he couldn't make out the numbers but he wasn't really looking for them, either.

While Jack was driving around the accident, another bump was heard in the back of the van.

"Shit," muttered Tony.

"Be cool, be cool" whispered Jack. He realized that the chloroform may be wearing off allowing their cargo to wake up. The cop continued to wave them through. Eventually the van rounded the accident, returned to the right lane and accelerated gradually.

"Man," Tony said with a sigh of relief. Jack drove on around the next bend in the road and took the last draw from his cigarette, rolled down the window and threw it out.

"See, we're alright." Jack said.

"Jesus fucking Christ." Tony muttered.

"Now go back there and see what the hell is happening." Jack said. "Tell her she better be the fuck quiet."

"Alright, just don't hit the goddam brakes this time," whined Tony.

CHAPTER 4

Tom followed Captain Wilson's patrol car to the sheriff's department in the town of Walterboro, South Carolina. When they arrived Wilson led them to a small room where he told them to make themselves comfortable and asked them if he could get them anything.

"Yes," Tom said. Could we get a couple of towels and some coffee?"

"Sure," Wilson said. "I'll be right back." Wilson closed the door. Rachel had settled down a little on the way to the sheriff's office, but now she seemed to become upset again.

"Hold on, baby." Tom Clark said to his wife as he held her tightly. "They will find her, O.K. They have to find her. It's just a matter of time." Rachel heard what her husband was saying but in her heart she was afraid that she would never see her beautiful daughter again.

"But wha....what if they don't?" She said, crying the words. She was crying now so hard she could barely speak. Melissa looked at her mother and began to cry also. She had never seen her mother that upset. Melissa was not old enough to comprehend all that was going on around her, but she knew that her mother was terribly upset and it upset her.

Tom Clark was nearly paralyzed with fear but he knew he had to be strong for his family. He was completely torn inside. He wanted so badly to be out with the searchers looking for his daughter. But, at the same time his wife and young daughter needed him too. Tom held them tightly while his insides were being tied in knots. Soon the door opened and Captain Wilson came in with some towels. He was followed by a female officer with two cups of coffee and a can of soda.

"Here you go." Wilson said. "You guys dry yourselves and have some coffee." Tom Clark took the towels and wrapped one around Rachel's shoulders and then wrapped one around Melissa. He got up from his seat and put Melissa beside her mother. He stepped over to Wilson.

"What are we doing to find my daughter?" he asked bluntly. Captain Wilson looked at the man standing in front of him and felt a little of the tremendous fear the man was obviously feeling. He felt a little helpless but he knew that he had to be careful dealing with their emotions. He'd had lots of experience with people who had lost loved ones for many different reasons. He would not want to get their hopes up but he did not want them to sink into despair, either.

"Mr. Clark, at this time all we can do is wait," he finally said. "We are mobilizing all of our available units and requesting assistance from neighboring counties." The man stared at him as if he did not hear him. Then he dropped his head a little.

"Is there anything I can do?" He said slowly, and then he looked into Wilson's eyes hard. "I have to get my daughter back." His lips trembled and tears welled in his eyes. "Is there anything I can do?" he said emphatically. Wilson stood silently considering the man's question, his situation. He had no answer that wouldn't sound stupid. He just put his hand on Tom's shoulder and shook his head.

"No, your wife and daughter need you here with them." Wilson said with a tone of urgency. "I will ensure that everything that can be done will be done to find your little girl." Tom looked into Wilson's eyes hoping to see truth in what he had said. Finally he nodded his head slowly and sat down beside his wife and Melissa and put his arms around them. He laid his head on Rachel's arm and cried.

* * * * * * *

Earlier the same day at Pops Marina, a small rundown marina on the Intracoastal Waterway near Beaufort, the boat in slip thirty-two had received a delivery. The captain of the boat was expecting one more delivery before he could sail. This last one was scheduled to arrive between ten p.m. and two in the morning. The owner and captain of the U.S. registered My Marie normally ran fishing charters out of Murrells Inlet, a little coastal town located just south of the Grand Strand and Myrtle Beach. It was famous for its seafood restaurants.

When the tourist business slowed at the end of the season, boat owners either tied up and waited for spring or took advantage of alternate means of support, some legal, some not so legal. Tillman Darby was tightening a valve cover bolt on the right bank on one of the two V8 diesel engines. He was attempting to slow a seeping oil leak when he heard footsteps on the wooden dock.

Darby is tall and muscular and well tanned from working in the sun. His hair was a dirty blond and hung shaggily just above his shoulders. On the boat he usually wore cutoff jean shorts and a sleeveless, white tee-shirt as he did today. He kept his boat spotless with little help from anyone else. During the fishing season he paid for the services of a deck hand to help keep an eye on the tourists who hired the My Marie to take them out to the gulfstream to fish. He lived on the boat believing that a house or apartment would be a waste of money.

Laying down the wrench and the flashlight, Darby grabbed a rag, wiped his hands and crawled out of the engine compartment. Emerging from the rear cabin into the salon, he looked around for the owner of the footsteps. Catching movement out of the corner of his eye, he glanced aft and noticed a figure on the dock waving his hand. Darby opened the door and walked back toward the figure. As he got closer he recognized the face as one he had seen before, on a previous charter of this sort.

"Hi." Tony Means whispered, looking around nervously. The insufficient lighting provided by the marina consisted of a couple of one-hundred watt bulbs hung ten to twelve feet apart from a wire strung down the length of the dock.

"Hello." Darby said tentatively. "You got something for me?"

"Yea man. Is it O.K. to bring it on down?" Tony asked still looking around the marina.

"Back your car up to the end of the dock and you'll have some cover. Take this cart here." Darby said pointing to a small cargo cart next to the boat. "Act like you're loading for a fishing trip and roll it on down, I'll wait here." Tony took the cart and pushed it up the wooden dock. He left it at the end of the dock and walked over to the driver's side of the van where Jack sat behind the wheel.

"Just back the van over there to the dock, I got a cart." Tony said.

"Who's down there?" Jack asked, concerned.

"I seen him before, on the first job I think, can't remember his name."

"Alright, move." Jack ordered, not wanting to run over Tony again. He pulled the van forward, then reversed and backed to the position Tony had pointed out. Jack got out of the van, quietly closed the door then walked to the front of the van and looked around. His feet crunched lightly on the gravel in the parking lot. He noticed the poor lighting and the secluded location. He looked over at the small building behind the opposite end on the marina. The lights were not on and there appeared to be no one there.

"Good choice," Jack thought to himself. He stepped around to the rear of the van and found Tony waiting. Jack slipped the key into the right door keyhole, rotated the key counter-clockwise and the lock clicked. He then grabbed the handle, pushed the chrome button and opened the door swinging it out to the right. He reached down to the in-side of the left door and released it and swung it open. The cargo began to move and almost fell out onto the ground until Jack moved forward and blocked the opening with his legs. A muffled cry was audible from under the tarp.

To the kidnappers, the little girl was just cargo. A product they were supplying to satisfy the demand of someone they would never meet. They learned to ask no questions. There would be no answers: Just do what you're told. In about ten minutes they would be in the clear, the cargo delivered and they would be on their way. The money would be delivered to Jack's house in a few days and then they'd wait for the next assignment.

Tony pushed the cart to the rear of the van while Jack grabbed the bundle and tightened the tarp around the girl. She moaned and tried to scream. A length of blonde hair fell out of the end of the bundle.

"Be quiet and everything will be O.K.. Don't make me angry." Jack whispered into the bundle in a menacing tone as he lowered it into the cart. Jack pushed her legs into a bent position so they wouldn't stick out of the end of the cart. Tony turned the cart around and rolled it down the dock to the boat while Jack walked beside with his hand holding the girl down. As they approached Darby, Jack nodded. He did not remember his name either and that was probably for the best. When they reached the boat, Jack reached down and removed the bundle from the cart and stepped up into the boat as the others kept an eye on the marina to be certain no one else was around. Jack followed Darby down to the forward cabin. Darby opened the door and turned on the light. Inside, the room was bare, except for the four girls sitting along the walls. Each had a set of chains attached to their wrists and ankles. Each one also had a small sack over their heads. Jack noticed that they were surprisingly motionless, probably drugged, or certainly they were sedated in some way.

Jack also noticed that they seemed to be young girls, but the one he brought was probably the youngest. He put her down where Darby indicated. They removed the tarp and then quickly attached the manacles that were reserved for that location on the wall. The girl had a cloth tied around her mouth and could only manage muffled attempts at protest. The two men avoided eye contact with the girl, which was the only real means of communication she had.

Audrey had been crying for hours, terrified, her eyes were begging for the two men to return her to her mother. Suddenly, all went dark as she felt something being pulled over her head and tightened around her neck. Audrey was numb with fear. She had awakened lying on cold crusty carpet covered in a mildewed tarp, and the odor had nearly made her sick. Her hands and legs were tied. Her head hurt. She had a terrible, chemical taste in her mouth. She thought that she was having a nightmare, but she quickly realized she was not dreaming. She was hurting too bad to be dreaming. It had only been two hours since she was violently ripped from her familiar life, but she really had no idea how long it had been.

"Have I been like this for hours or days?" Audrey tried to think. The chemical had confused her. Time had been disrupted for her. All she knew for certain was that she was sitting among other people and bound by chains. She could not see and she could not stop crying. "What is happening to me? What is happening to me?" She cried to her self. Soon she heard the men leave the room. But she felt the presence of the other girls in the little room with her. She could not see them but she could hear the small noises they made. All was silent except for the occasional moan from one of the other people in the room with her. She began to struggle at her bindings but the metal hurt her wrists when she tested the bindings.

Suddenly she heard the door open followed by someone entering the room. She stopped moving. A strong hand grabbed her arm, she resisted but the hand was far stronger than her feeble resistance. He was hurting her. She protested to no avail. Then she felt a sharp sting on the inside of her forearm. She realized someone was giving her a shot. She cried. Soon she began to feel relaxed, sleepy, she drifted off, and as she did she tried to call her mother. "Mommy? Mom?" She called as strongly as she could through the cloth in her mouth. But her attempt to say her mothers' name trailed off as she slipped into a deep sleep.

CHAPTER 5

Russell Stone was in his office lifting weights when the phone rang. He learned a long time ago that maintaining a good physical condition was a requirement for his job, especially as the years began to add up. He hated to be interrupted while he was working out. Once he got into the zone he didn't want any interference, especially a phone call.

"I should have taken the damn thing off the hook." He mumbled through gritted teeth caused by the strain of the barbell. Russ, as his friends and relatives knew him, began his career in the United States Army. He had not been able to afford college after high school and his grades had not been so good, although his military entrance exams revealed an impressive I.Q. Russ had excelled in sports in high school to the detriment of his studies. He had been voted captain of both the football and track team. He felt he could have played football for many of the smaller colleges and he tried out for a few. College football coaches tended to concentrate on recruiting players from teams with good records and the players with the right numbers. Russ' weight and height didn't draw much attention and his high school teams' record in his final season was unimpressive.

Unfortunately, the college coaches missed the opportunity to recruit a player with heart and a natural ability in leadership. Unable to be accepted as a regular student and then "walk on" due to his grades, Russ decided to let the Army provide his education. He opted to be a "real" soldier by joining the infantry and requesting the Special Forces. After basic training at Ft. Jackson, South Carolina, Russ attended Special Forces training at Ft. Bragg in North Carolina and Jump School at Ft. Benning, Georgia, graduating with honors from both.

Russ understood the need to have a degree, so he attended college at night on the Army's nickel, completing his bachelor's degree in criminal justice in four years, even with several training deployments to Europe and as a squad leader in Desert Storm. Six years later, Russ left the Army but not without a recruiting attempt by Delta Force, who also had their headquarters at Ft. Bragg. Staff Sergeant Stone would be sent to Officers Candidate School, commissioned a second lieutenant and assigned an assistant team leader. But SSgt. Stone decided to go back home and take a position with the sheriffs department.

A friend on the force had known of Russ' education in criminal justice and knew that the sheriffs department was growing and needed someone with Russ' abilities. He enjoyed his time in the military but making it a career was never his intention. He had gotten what he wanted and the Army had gotten his services at an extremely good price. Russ applied for the position and it was offered to him. He was glad to get back home. He found a home in the missing persons section and made a name for himself in the investigation of several cases.

Since the FBI becomes involved early in most missing persons cases, Russ became known to many in the agency. So it was a natural move when he accepted a position with the FBI's National Center for the Analysis of Violent Crime (NCAVC), which is part of the FBI's Critical Incident Response Group. NCAVC maintains Evidence Response Teams (ERT's), which conduct evidence recovery operations at crime scenes in support of federal, state, and local law enforcement agencies. ERT's are tasked to provide assistance in a variety of crime scenes. Such a team had been dispatched to South Carolina in support of the investigation of the disappearance of Audrey Clark.

Special Agent Stone and his team specialized in kidnapping and hostage cases. Stone developed an intense interest in the investigation and recovery of missing persons. He seemed to have a sixth sense when he investigated a missing persons case. Soon after arriving at the FBI

Russ stumbled over an old case that had not been solved. He reopened the investigation even though many of his colleagues told him he would be wasting his time. A sixteen year old girl had vanished on her way to school, no witnesses, and no evidence. Russ worked on the case in his spare time and managed to tease out a new suspect. A registered sex offender who lived near her home town had been questioned but released when he produced an alibi. The FBI worked on the case for three years with no result. Russ managed to get information that put the sex offenders alibi in question and a warrant was issued to search the mans residence. The girls' remains were unearthed in his back yard. The man was convicted and received four life sentences for the crime.

Russ' peers as well as his superiors in the bureau admired his many successes. But, there seemed to be a percentage of cases that led nowhere. No matter how hard he worked on a case, there was no trail, no witnesses or evidence. The victim just seemed to vanish. These cases troubled Russ Stone. After a period of time his supervisors would require Stone to move on to new cases. He was forced to file away the unsolved case. Leaving someone in this status did not sit well with him. People had lost a loved one and he had no idea what happened to them. He began to take these cases personally, working on them on his own time, after normal business hours, as he had done with the missing sixteen year old girl.

He began to see a pattern among many of the cases. There was no reason for these people to go missing. There was no divorce involved or there was no conflict among the divorced parents. There was no business or personal relationships that had gone bad. Romantic relationships were not strained. Most of the victims of these cases were female. They were usually well-balanced, happy girls from happy families. There was no logical reason for them to be missing.

After ten years with the FBI, Russ realized the limitations inherent in such a large organization with such a huge bureaucracy. He felt that he could be more effective solo. Besides, he had become extremely frustrated with the red tape and the childish behavior of "lifers" with the hope of retirement and maintaining their inflated egos being their only motivation. A private citizen not bound by departmental rules and regulations, Russ functioned alone for the sake of effectiveness. The enjoyment of helping to locate missing persons at the sheriff's department and later at the FBI caused his defection to the ranks of consultant, a name not exactly accurate or preferred but it worked for his accountant. Consultant was preferable to Private Investigator, a group of people not overly admired by professional law enforcement, primarily because of the lack of training. This training deficit tended to cause trouble for the professionally trained Sheriff or municipal law enforcement officers.

Russ Stone had become accustomed to the intermissions between cases, a state that had been difficult to achieve due to the habits developed in the Special Forces, sheriffs department and at the FBI. The need for robot-like personal efficiency had been replaced by an ability to have all of life's details ordered in such a way that he could pick up and leave once the phone hit the cradle. A skill that was needed now, with the phone going off while one hundred and fifty pounds was making its way up the full length of his arms extension for the fourteenth time. Dropping the bar into the rack, he sat up, wiped his face and grabbed the phone; placing the handset to his ear he heard a familiar voice half shouting his name. Russ knew before the last vocalization of his name who had uttered it. William Barnes had become a close friend over the past few years. He was an assistant director in the missing persons section at Quantico. Invariably, after the FBI has exhausted its resources in an effort to locate a missing person, a family member was not satisfied and was willing to fund an independent attempt to find their loved one.

One of the most difficult elements of the job is the initial contact with the family member. The father, mother, husband or wife is unwilling to accept the possibility that they may never see the loved one again. It is important to not think in such terms as "missing individual," when the person is a close family member of the client. If the case is accepted, and many aren't, it is absolutely necessary to have the proper relationship with the client. An offended client will not be as helpful because of the lack of trust that will result. Bill Barnes has a special ability to be able to recognize a case with potential for positive outcome. He was able to evaluate the client and be fairly certain that they have the ability to follow through and tolerate the ups and downs and possible negative outcome of a protracted effort to locate the missing loved one.

"Russ, are you there?" Bill half yelled into the phone.

"Yea, Yea, man, just give me a second to catch my breath." Russ said as he wiped the sweat from his face, and tried to catch his breath. "O.K., Whatcha got?"

"I faxed you a case I thought you may want to look at. Unfortunately, we can't put any more time in it and I mentioned you to the family and they would like you to consider taking the case." Bill said, a little more relaxed.

"What is the short version?" Russ asked between breaths.

"Typical…. Girl grabbed from the family's car at an interstate rest-stop down in South Carolina." Barnes said.

"Ransom?" Stone asked.

"No, just vanished, no trace, there has been no contact with the family. We did the usual workup. Sent a team, but got nowhere. Same as the other recent grabs… don't know if it's a serial killer, slave trader or alien abductions," Bill said with a tone of frustration.

"I'll call Mulder and see if there are any aliens active in the Bible Belt." Russ retorted with a grin, knowing how real agents get irritated with such comments comparing real cops to TV cops.

"You do that, Russ and while you're at it call Ace Ventura and get his opinion." Bill countered.

"O.K. just kidding, relax." Russ said.

"This is a tough one, nice family, shouldn't happen to people like this. Winos and runaways are different, you know, they are asking for trouble. This girl was just sitting in the family car waiting for her parents to use the restroom." Barnes was silent for a moment as if considering the case. "Well, let me know if I can be of any help if you take it." Bill concluded.

"Thanks, I'll let you know, see ya." Russ reached over and hung up the phone, as he did he glanced at his own family in the picture on the desk. Yes, he could imagine what it would be like for his son or daughter to be gone. That was what drove him, an idea that if he could put these people out of business, they would not be able to do this to anyone he loved.

The memories of several particularly tragic cases were never far from his conscious thought. The effect of finding a child mutilated by a monster who is only technically categorized as a human being, after becoming personally close to the family through the investigation cannot be described verbally. But, unfortunately, the parents would rather know what happened. It is an acceptable risk in the effort to find the child. Most parents are willing to suffer the possibility of the worst outcome to have any chance of finding their child.

Russ got up from the weight bench and walked over to his desk. He punched the space bar on the PC to clear the screensaver. He clicked the fax icon. As the window opened, he noticed his wife in the backyard cleaning up around the pool. The kids had their friends over for the weekend and there were still floats and toys lying about. He checked the time and realized that she would be leaving soon to pick up Jake and Amanda from their respective schools. Russ dried more sweat from his head and face as he clicked on the new file. The pages that opened on the screen were in the familiar format of the FBI. He clicked on the print icon and headed for the shower while the pages printed out.

Emerging from the bathroom after a much needed shower, Russ noticed that the last page sitting in the printer tray was a picture of the missing girl. Picking up the stack of sheets he felt the familiar pain as the image of the girl burned into his memory. She was a pretty little girl with long blonde hair. In the picture she was smiling and obviously very happy. He reversed the order of the sheets and then read them.

The data was organized in his mind and sorted and compared to previous experience. He recognized a familiar feeling in the pit of his stomach, a convergence of emotions, one positive, the other of dread. He realized that there may be little chance of a positive outcome in this case considering the thorough investigation performed by all agencies involved. At least he doesn't have to ask the difficult questions of parents who would be in a state of shock. His entry would come at a time when many parents are near the point of acceptance that they may never see their child again. It is important that he not create false expectations and interrupt any emotional healing that may have occurred.

Russ decided that he would contact Tom and Rachel Clark and set up a meeting. His decision to take the case would not be made until he spoke to the parents face to face. He had to be certain that they would be supportive and able to handle the stress that would be a part of the work Russ would need to do.

CHAPTER 6

The morning after accepting the last delivery scheduled at the little marina near Beaufort, Darby was up early making the boat ready to sail. The fuel tanks had been topped off upon arriving, after tying up at his assigned slip. Darby rechecked the engine compartment to be certain every thing was secure. Taking his position behind the wheel, Darby flipped the switch that turned on the exhaust fans that vented any lingering fuel vapors from the engine compartment. He then activated the switch that sends voltage to the glow plugs of the two diesel engines. When the light went out signifying the combustion chambers had reached their proper temperature, he pushed the starter button sending voltage to the starter motor on the first engine. The engine fired and Darby released the starter button. He repeated the process for the second engine. He monitored the engines for a minute or so until they had settled into a smooth idle and then he left the helm to secure the fore and aft mooring lines. He returned to the helm and engaged the drive. He increased the RPM's until he was moving forward at the required speed. Darby slowly steered the My Marie away from the dock and through a couple of narrow passages and into the Intracoastal Waterway. His plan was to follow the waterway south, ultimately to Ft. Pierce, Florida where another pickup was scheduled. In the meantime, his job would be to keep a low profile and to keep his cargo alive.

Movements of the type of boat Darby piloted are typical of the boats seen on the Intracoastal Waterway and as far out as the Gulf Stream on fishing charters. During the off season, if there was not enough demand for charters at their home ports, these boats would move south to the ports on Florida's coast. The course of My Marie would not cause any concern for the Coast Guard or any harbor patrols as long as Darby did not bring any attention to himself by violating any maritime laws. All registration and insurance requirements were up to date. The boat had its Coast Guard inspection within the past year. There should be no red flags in the event that My Marie's registration records were accessed. Movements of boats along the southeast and gulf coasts had become increasingly the concern of the DEA with the growth of the drug trade. Drug smugglers had become very ingenious in their operations requiring the DEA and other agencies to tighten security along the United States coastlines.

Darby would have to stop periodically to refuel and replenish supplies. The cargo would be inspected, fed and drugged. He had perfected the process of providing restroom breaks for the "passengers," an unpleasant process due to the emotional and physical control that had to be maintained over his unwilling charges.

As long as the weather held up, the trip would take no more than the planned five days. Darby would make the first leg alone. A stop in Savannah included picking up a crewman to help with food and restroom breaks. It was imperative that the cargo arrive at its destination in good health. Medical attention was not planned for and if needed might simply result in the affected cargo being discarded overboard. This action was of course a last resort since it was more profitable to keep the cargo healthy and deliver the full load.

"She seems to be running normally." Darby thought to himself. This trip would provide the cash needed to get her ready for the next charter season. The engine needed work and she needed to be hauled out and the hull cleaned and refinished. He would have had plenty of money from this summer's work, but any extra money he may have had was spent on a very active nightlife and a new car. He was not completely comfortable with the part-time work he had found, or that found him, as it were. His recruitment had been subtle. One night, while donating a large portion of the day's charter revenue to his favorite local nightclub, an acquaintance had given him a piece of paper with a phone number on it. He told Darby that a man had asked about the My Marie and wanted to hire her. Neither Darby nor his friend knew the man. He made the phone call and a deal was made. Darby had only talked to his contact over the phone. As soon as the contact had gotten Darby's phone number, the number Darby was given was disconnected. At the time this seemed strange to him, but now he understands the need for security. His time in the Navy had instilled in him the idea of operations security, so he was well prepared for this type of assignment. It really seemed to be too clean though. How did they know that he would be willing to enter into this kind of work? The contact had a lot of personal information on Darby and he was informed in no uncertain terms that security would be enforced, meaning exactly what it sounded like. Darby was not married, but his parents were still alive and living in Conway, South Carolina. He had a brother and a sister, both married, with children and lived normal lives compared to his. He was convinced that the location and daily activities of his close relatives were contained in a dossier on someone's desk.

Darby steered the boat while monitoring the depth sounder and the GPS. He glanced periodically at the chart to be certain of his position relative to the course he intended to make. He began to wonder who the passengers were, where they came from. He knew how they got to his boat but what would happen to them when he delivered them to the port on Grand Bahama island. He was just one cog in a very efficient piece of machinery. Nobody knew anything except for his or her little part. In fact, an intelligent person would understand that it is safer if nobody else involved in this game knows your name. If you are unknown to others, then you can remain unknown to the authorities if they become involved.

CHAPTER 7

Azim Abdulah Rahhim sat at a table outside of the café two blocks from his flat in Paris where he had breakfast most mornings. It was a clear day and the food had been excellent as usual. Rahhim was dressed well as always. There was no room for less than the finest for him any longer. Today he was wearing a custom tailored black suit that matched his black neatly trimmed hair. His Italian loafers and socks were black as well. His white linen shirt was the only white item he wore. Several gold rings and a gold chain adorned his fingers and neck. Rahhim had a stocky build but he was not fat. He maintained a membership in a local men's club and worked out several times a week. His face was dark, an indication of his ancestry. He had a square jaw and black piercing eyes. He was always clean shaven.

He had become accustom to the finer things in life. Tolerating inferior service wasn't necessary when the best can be obtained regardless of price. Since making Paris his home, he had come to appreciate certain aspects of the western lifestyle. He was a native of the Sudan. He only returned to his homeland when business forced him to do so. Otherwise, he was happier to leave the problems of the Sudan to those who chose to stay there and deal with them. Paul Rahhim, an alias taken for use in the West, had transformed a tradition practiced in his homeland and applied it to the western capitalist economy and in the process became a wealthy man. The ability to function in his chosen profession was due to the conditioning he received growing up in Africa where trade in human beings had been a normal part of life for centuries.

Rahhims' clients included the enormously wealthy from all over the world; men and women who were able to pay any amount for the things they desired. Extreme wealth also allowed for the privacy that was necessary for the participation in many of their more perverse and usually illegal desires. Rahhims' clients were comfortable doing business with him because of his discretion. He was a man of considerable experience in all of the important cultures of the world. He was fluent in English, French and Arabic. His education was impeccable, as was his effectiveness in satisfying the needs of his eminent clients.

The weather in Paris was getting progressively cooler as the end of summer neared. Another few weeks and he would be forced to take his meals inside. Autos zipped by on the narrow street in front of the café. Drivers participated in the daily game of going to work, going to lunch, back to work and then home, day after day. The only exception to the monotony of life in the city was the annual vacations and the many holidays provided France's socialist policies. Rahhim was thankful that he had been able to excuse himself from that mundane ritual. Due to his ability to create an effective network of operatives throughout the world, he has the luxury of being anonymous and detached from the legwork of his troops on the ground. Operatives, most of whom have never seen him, would not know him if he were standing next to him. His organization had been operating with the efficiency of a well run fortune five hundred company for over ten years, and had made Rahhim a very wealthy man.

Rahhim paid for his meal and left his usual generous tip. He exited the café and made his way toward his flat, lost among the other Parisians, who all seemed to be moving a little swifter than Rahhim. He stopped at a newsstand and picked up his daily copy of La Monde. He scanned the headlines on the first page, folded it, tucked it under his arm and turned toward his flat. A few minutes later he was standing outside of his building. He opened his mailbox and removed three letters from the box. He locked the box and walked up the stairwell. The accommodations here were pleasant. He had one of the largest apartments for the money in Paris. He could live just about anywhere he wanted, but his western indoctrination did not alleviate a certain sense of thrift he aquired while growing up in the Sudan.

His father had been an officer in the Sudanese Army who had seen a lot of action in the conflicts with the north. His mother, a school teacher, loved her son and wished that she could have removed him from the continent that seemed to be in constant turmoil. But his father's career had prevented that. The family lived comfortably, although modestly on the salaries of a Sudanese Army officer and a teacher. They were among the small minority of the population of the Sudan that had money and lived better than most. But Rahhim was surrounded by poverty while he was growing up. He did not have to travel very far from home to witness the extreme poverty so prevalent in sub-Saharan Africa. His family had to be careful to guard their relative success. The ease of losing everything was very common in the Sudan; his parents had instilled a fairly conservative mindset in the young Rahhim.

Ironically, the southern parts of the Sudan had been the beneficiary of colonial exploitation by old European powers. The process had allowed the southern part of the country to develop quicker economically and socially leaving the north to stagnate. The northern part of the country was primarily agricultural and had remained that way. The education received by the children in the north was so inferior to that in the south that it created such a divergence in the standard of living that civil war had eventually consumed the nation. Rahhim grew up in this environment. During this time he learned many of the skills he put to use in building his empire. The most important knowledge he would gain was the demand for the product he would grow wealthy providing to an eager, though small market. His product was slaves.

Some questioned whether prostitution was the oldest profession. Some scholars believed that the oldest profession was actually slave trading. In many cases the two were one in the same. The practice of slavery had existed in almost every culture in recorded history. The earliest writings of human existence reflected this practice. Slavery was common to distinct cultures around the globe. Human cultures separated by vast distances exhibited a common legacy, the exploitation of groups of people for the benefit of another in one form or another. Many third world countries were still actively participating in this ancient custom. Efforts by international agencies were limited in their ability to stem slavery activities in these countries due to the unofficial support of the governments. In addition to the Sudan, slavery was practiced in Chad, Libya and most Persian Gulf states. The Koran prohibited its followers from owning fellow Muslims, but it did not provide the same protection for followers of other religions. The Bible contains passages referring to owning slaves as a normal part of life. The Jews, having been slaves themselves, are admonished to treat their slaves humanely.

Women and children in these countries could be bought and sold for as little as the equivalent of fifty American dollars. In Asia, girls were sold into slavery and forced into prostitution. It was estimated that ten million people were trapped in debt bondage in India, which was the practice of providing money to the family or paying off debts the family owed and taking a child to work in the household to payoff the amount owed. The child was actually never able to earn freedom because the debt continued to increase by charging room, board and other costs. Less publicized was the holding of slaves brought in from western countries by Rahhim and others like him for wealthy individuals in private residences. Most people were familiar with the many "residences" Saddam Hussein had spread across Iraq but few knew the truth of what went on behind those walls. Access was strictly limited to those residences. It was thought this was due to military secrets but the presence of indentured servants held against their will was just as likely.

* * * * * * *

The weather along the Georgia and Florida coast was beautiful. Darby had little trouble navigating the Intracoastal Waterway on his way to Ft. Pierce. The new crewman he picked up in Savannah had worked out well. He kept his mouth shut and did as he was told. Darby believed him to be Cuban but he was not certain. Darby spoke no Spanish and Miquel understood only enough English to get by. Miquel was "assigned" to help Darby on this voyage. He may be just earning his way to Freeport as he will disembark there and be on his way.

"That's fine," thought Darby, for he only needed the help on this leg of the voyage. The helm required Darby's full attention while in the waterway. Out in open ocean, the autopilot could be set and the captain could take care of other things aboard the vessel. The waterway was fairly busy for this time of year. He encountered many boats that appeared to be moving to warmer ports for the winter. He noticed a lot of New England city names on the transoms of boats headed in his direction. Darby checked his fuel gauge and calculated there was enough fuel to make it to nightfall. He looked at his chart and located a small marina within range and made a mental note to stop there, refuel and sleep for the night. Darby turned as he heard a noise. Miquel appeared from the door leading below.

"Girls make noise." Miquel said in his limited English vocabulary. Darby had thought he heard thumping noises earlier. He looked at Miquel to try to be clear.

"Find out which one. She might need to use the head, O.K.?" Darby said slowly, trying to be understood.

"O.K." Miquel replied. Darby had explained the procedures for the trips to the head to Miquel shortly after he boarded in Savannah. He would come back to get him to help if he thought the noisy girl needed to relieve herself. The shots he was administering to them would keep them groggy for eight hours. They still had a few hours before he would have to readminister the shots. He realized from previous experience that the girls would begin to tolerate the drug and he would have to move the doses to every seven hours and then to six. But the man who had trained him to use the drug told him not to give it less than six hours apart. After a few minutes Miquel popped up though the doorway.

"Girl says she has to go." Miquel mumbled.

"Alright." Darby said shaking his head. " I'll stop as soon as I can." Darby noticed a widening of the waterway just beyond a bridge in the distance. He decided to stop there for a break. There were a few other things he could take care of anyway. They might as well go ahead and feed them and give them all toilet breaks while they were stopped. Then he could continue nonstop to the marina for fuel. He would be docking in Ft. Pierce the next day as planned. He would receive the last delivery the next evening. The morning after that he would be on his way to Freeport.

* * * * * * *

Paul Rahhim was known for his ability to satisfy unique requirements. "Special" requests were not difficult to fill, although the clients were never informed of the ease of fulfillment, thus justifying the high value placed on the product. He unlocked the door to his flat, walked over to his desk and laid down the mail. After removing his jacket, he sat down and turned on his laptop to retrieve any email that may have been received since the night before. The list of new email revealed only two important communications. The rest were deleted without review. Based on the senders' addresses, he knew they would be encrypted, so he opened them within the encryption software. The first message simply stated that six hundred and fifty thousand in American funds were received at his Swiss bank and were deposited in his numbered account per his instructions. The second message was less straightforward. It said simply, "Five packages in warehouse. One more to be delivered tomorrow P.M."

Rahhim sat at his desk and composed a message, encrypted it and transmitted it. The addressee was an unremarkable one, and useless unless you were able to track it through the many servers it was routed through and resent with new addresses in order to disguise its ultimate destination and its originator. In this case the location of the ultimate destination was a server beside the desk of an administrative assistant of a walled and guarded estate ten miles northeast of the city limits of Damascus, Syria.

* * * * * * *

The weather deteriorated as the My Marie approached Ft. Pierce before sunrise the following morning. The rain came down hard and Darby was required to find calm water and wait out the storm. He and Miquel buttoned up the vessel to make it as watertight as possible. The swells in the waterway were as bad as Darby had ever seen. He checked the anchors. They seemed to be holding. The wind was blowing from the south-west. Darby had positioned the boat so that it would blow away from the right bank of the waterway. As long as the anchors held, all should be fine. Miquel was sitting on the couch in the cabin and seemed not to be worried about the storm. He appeared to be on the verge of sleep. The beer bottle was about to slip from his hand. Darby took it from him and put it in the sink. He realized that the rocking of the boat could cause seasickness so he went below and opened the door to the forward cabin. All of the girls seemed to be asleep. He walked over and one by one he raised the hood on each head. The shots were working well; they didn't seem to be aware of the rolling of the vessel or that there was even a storm. Darby lowered the hood on the last girl and left the room. "Good time to get a little shut-eye." Darby thought to himself. He went into the rear cabin and stretched out on the small bed and closed his eyes. The rocking of the boat helped ease him into a deep sleep.

CHAPTER 8

The 757 descended through the clouds from twelve thousand feet on its final approach to Atlanta's Hartsfield International Airport. Russ' flight from Ronald Reagan had been uneventful. Russ tensed as he felt the wheels touch down separately and the plane seemed to swerve subtly to the right, evidently compensating for a crosswind. Russ Stone's stomach twitched. Only when the nose wheel confidently made contact with the runway did the airplane feel properly lined up and rolling straight. Russ' neck muscles relaxed and he exhaled the breath that he didn't realize he was holding. Thankful to be on solid ground, he made his way to collect his luggage and then to the taxi stand for a ride over to Tom Clark's office building in the Buckhead section of Atlanta.

Following a harried ride though Atlanta, the taxi finally reached the office building identified on Russ' hand scribbled note. Exiting the cab, he paid the cabby and headed for the entrance in search of the elevator. Russ wondered when Atlanta had become as dangerous to travel in as New York. He was just here a few years ago and didn't remember fearing for his life on that visit. Maybe he was just getting older and understood that considering how lucky he had been never to be seriously injured in military action or on the streets of a bustling city, maybe his luck would soon run out. "It's a karma thing." Russ thought. He had to be more careful these days.

He quickly located the set of elevators. A few seconds after pushing the up button between the two elevators, the doors opened and he got on. When he reached his floor, the doors whined open to reveal three people waiting to get on. Russ exited and searched for the office number where he would find Tom Clark. The office door was glass and Russ could see a receptionist sitting at a desk just inside. Russ entered and was refreshed by the warm smile of the attractive receptionist who greeted him. After a few pleasantries, she excused herself and walked back to Clark's office to announce Stones arrival. She had just gotten out of view when Russ was startled by a man nearly running to greet him. Tom Clark quickly introduced himself and ushered him into his office where Russ was glad to find a comfortable chair to finally relax in. A matching armchair was beside Russ' and Tom settled into that one, a more friendly position than being seated behind the desk. Tom Clark was dressed in a well fitting suit and his office was neat and clean. Russ noticed several pictures of Tom's family on his desk and walls.

"Thank you very much for coming." Tom said, sounding sincere and sorrowful at the same time.

"Your welcome," assured Russ. "How are you and Rachel doing?"

"O.K., I guess," Tom hesitated a moment, "we are both back to work. We were not being very productive at home." Tom said.

"I know how stressful this can be, I've seen others in this position and you guys seem to be handling the situation as well as can be expected."

"It's been eight days, and I really expect one of us to crack soon," Tom admitted. "Rachel has begun therapy but she is threatening to stop. I have had to insist that she continue but I'm afraid I may have to join her soon." Tom said, barely containing his emotions. Tom hesitated for a moment as if trying to choose his words carefully. "Can you help us?" he muttered looking directly into Russ' eyes.

Russ had lied. He knew he couldn't possibly understand what the two of them were going through. He had witnessed many such men in the same position, but empathy can only reveal the shallow layers of the pain felt by a person in this situation. Most of the men he had met having lost a child eventually sunk into a deep depression or worse. Some recovered, some did not. He was thankful that he hadn't been there. He was afraid of how he may react. Tom's composure was remarkable.

"I will do all that I can." Russ answered. "I have a lot of work to do and it might only get worse for you and your family. If we do find your daughter it will be only after much stress and fear." Russ continued. "If you and Rachel are able to be strong and hopeful, then we have the best chance of success. I need you to be available and lucid when I need you, for your daughters' sake." Russ concluded. Tom looked down at his hands and remained silent, and then looked over at Russ with tearful eyes.

"Please find her." Tom put his head in his hands trying to hold back his tears.. Russ remained silent recognizing the extreme pain Tom suffered. "I'm sorry." Tom said eventually. He held his head up and wiped his eyes with the back of his hand. After an awkward second or two, he regained his composure. "Let's go on over to the house, Rachel should be there soon. We can stop by your hotel so you can freshen up if you like."

"That sounds good, thanks." Russ said.

* * * * * * *

When Tom and Russ arrived at the Clark home, Rachel had already been there for several hours. She left work early to prepare for the arrival of the man she believed would find her daughter. Rachel still felt like it had all been a bad dream. She was forced to live this nightmare and follow the rules that this terrible dilemma had given her. She hoped soon to wake from the horror and find her daughter back home with her.

Her life had depended on routine. Just getting through the day, doing the things that were required and trying to do them well was difficult for her. At work she was more like a robot than the creative, productive professional that her colleagues were used to. They tried to understand and make allowances for her. At home, Rachel made herself busy around the house cleaning, rearranging, and cooking but rarely did she go into Audrey's room. She hoped that if she followed the rules and got her work done the terrible dream would end and she would be reunited with her precious daughter.

Rachel's mother, Angela, had been at their home since the abduction, except for returning to her own home to get the mail and feed the cat. Rachel's father had passed away five years before so she had the freedom to stay as long as she was needed. The two of them had cooked an ample meal and set up the spare room with the hope of Russ staying with them instead of the hotel. Rachel was inwardly motivated by a need to be aware of her primary motivation for her hospitality. Angela was surprised at the level Rachel was able to function. She did breakdown often, but it was usually in private or when she was alone with her or Tom. It had only been eight days since the abduction and Angela was afraid that Rachel's emotions would eventually overwhelm her and she would have to be hospitalized. So far though, she was controlling, or hiding her sorrow well. The need to return to work had been therapeutic. It seemed to have provided an outlet for her stress.

She had not revealed her true feelings though. She was convinced that Audrey's abduction was her fault, she should have been paying attention, and she should have locked the doors and watched the girls instead of napping. She also tried to convince herself that Audrey would be found and returned to her safe and sound, and she would awaken from her terrible dream.

It was not possible for her life to go on without her daughter. Audrey belonged here, safe at home. This was just a mistake and it would be corrected soon. It had to be. Rachel had forced herself to communicate with authorities, believing that she may be able to contribute to the effort to find Audrey. But more and more she recognized that little progress was being made. The local authorities in South Carolina seemed to be totally lost, only SLED and the FBI seemed to be competent, but they had not entered the investigation until three days had passed.

Considering the lack of success in the investigation, Rachel was holding up well. She was an intelligent woman and could evaluate the situation within the realm of reality and make accurate assessments. Since the abduction, Rachel didn't smile as much. She was not as fastidious in her appearance and her face was drawn from worry and lack of sleep. She was beginning to suspect that as time went on, the chances of finding Audrey got slimmer. "Russell Stone may be our last hope," she thought to herself as she rinsed the cooking utensils, placing each of them in the dishwasher. She had an analytical mind. She trusted Stone's experience, especially considering the recommendation given by the FBI Special Agent involved in the investigation. Rachel came to the realization of the possibility that if Stone didn't find her daughter, she might never see her again.

With that thought she began to cry just as she heard the front door open. She met Tom coming around the corner and she looked into his eyes. He realized she had been crying. He stopped and reached for her, they hugged tightly. Russ recognized the scene and stopped moving. Tom kissed her softly on the cheek and turned and introduced Russ and Rachel. Rachel reached for Russ' hand.

"I'm sorry, Mr. Stone, I was doing O.K. today until I was alone," she said.

"Please call me Russ, and I hope I would be as strong as you under the same circumstances," Russ said, trying to reassure her.

Rachel replied, "I'm trying. I don't know how long I can last though. Thank you for helping us. We are glad someone with your experience is willing to help." Russ took her hand and squeezed it lightly.

"I will do all that I can." He said. "As I told Tom, I just need you two to continue to be strong and do exactly as I say. We have a lot of work to do and the process will be stressful." He continued. "Just remember that my goal is to find your daughter and I will do my best, I promise." Russ said reassuringly.

"Thank you Russ, just tell us what we need to do." Tom said.

"Well," Russ said. "I believe someone has gone to some trouble to prepare dinner. I think we should not let it go to waste."

"You're right," said Rachel, as she turned toward the dining room, "I hope you like chicken and broccoli casserole?"

"I do, and I thought only my wife was aware of that combination."

Russ said with a slight laugh.

"She must have to try to get nutrients into young children? Rachel said.

"Yea, two. They are stubborn when it comes to eating good food-like most kids I assume." Russ answered. Just then Angela appeared from upstairs where she was getting Melissa ready for bed. Tom introduced Angela who thanked Russ for his willingness to help. They then moved into the dining room to begin dinner. They sat at the dining room table and began passing the food around so that each could get their share.

"Where is Melissa?" Russ asked after remembering that he needed to talk to her.

"She is upstairs in her room. My mother just put her to bed. Why?" Rachel asked.

"Well, I noticed in the reports I received from the ERT that she's the only one who actually saw the men who took Audrey." Russ answered.

"She says she saw one of them, but the other officers aren't sure how reliable her memory may be." Tom said.

"Well, I have found that children can be extremely helpful," assured Russ. "If you don't mind I'd like to talk with her before I leave Atlanta."

"O.K.," Rachel said. "If you think it will help."

"If she knows anything, it will help." Russ said. "I'm sure she wants her sister back as much as the rest of us."

* * * * * * *

The storm finally blew over and Darby found his marina in Ft. Pierce. He pulled out of the slip in Ft. Pierce shortly after taking delivery of the sixth "passenger." The trip to Freeport was uneventful. Darby and Miguel maintained the passengers and the vessel. Darby was still troubled by the constant oil leak, requiring him to spend more time than he liked in the engine compartment drying the oil and attempting to staunch its flow. Darby was up early the morning after docking in Freeport. With the cargo unloaded and transferred to his contact in the Bahamas, he could breathe a little easier. The delivery of the six items the previous evening had gone smoothly. The authorities in the Bahamas were not nearly as competent as those in the United States. Security was much less of a problem in the islands. He had no idea what would happen to the six girls from then on and he did not care to know either. His part of the operation was over, except for payment, which he expected in the mail when he arrived at his homeport in Murrells Inlet. He would much rather be running cocaine or grass in these waters than transporting human beings for reasons that he could only imagine. To Darby this was only business, but he didn't consider himself the kind of person that would intentionally hurt another human being without good reason. Unfortunately his "good reason" in this case was money. He felt a little sympathy for the girls he transported out of U.S. waters on their way to God knows where. He was glad he did not have to talk to any of them, the drugs made certain of that. He could easily be talked into setting them free. He knew that. Darby decided that he was better off just not thinking about those girls any longer. He would be setting sail soon for a small port on Great Abaco to pick up the cargo for the return trip. He wasn't sure yet whether it would be smoke or blow, he just knew he would not be as nervous handling his next load.

The engine should hold out until he could get back to West Palm, he hoped. He just had to get the maintenance done there before he headed back up the coast to Murrells Inlet. These runs would make the off-season profitable enough to get all repairs done for the tourist season. The legitimate business of taking vacationing Canadians and New Englanders out to the Gulf Stream to puke and bottom fish was much less risky than the off-season business he had developed over the years. After securing the vessel for sailing, he found himself once again cruising the open sea. The trip from Freeport to the little port on Great Abaco would only take six hours. At least this short sail would be free from carrying anything illegal and he could enjoy the cruising again the way he did when he began his business. In the beginning he was in it only for the enjoyment of the sea. Since then it had become a business and the goal had become to pay the bills and have enough money left over to party regularly. Leaving Grand Bahama Island, the My Marie headed east. The water was smooth and clear. The sky was free of threatening clouds and there was little wind. Dolphins escorted the 60 foot Bertram Sport Fisherman into deeper water, jumping at the bow. They didn't care what your mission was, they just wanted to play. The water was its normal crystal clear greenish-blue. The day was warm and sunny although the slight chill in the air confirmed that fall was just around the corner. The six-hour cruise would be relaxing.

* * * * * * *

Russ and the Clarks along with Rachel's mother, finished their meal and they retired to the living room where Russ intended to begin his debriefing of the Clarks. He had learned to be subtle and careful during this period because an upset witness was very little help. Russ began by simply inquiring into the family's normal activities. Where do the girls go to school? What extracurricular activities do they participate in? Who are their friends? What do they do during summer vacations? Russ assumed the kidnapping was one of simple opportunity but he did want to rule out any preexisting motives. Russ was able to learn a good deal about the Clarks during this informal meeting and at the same time he wanted to be certain that the three of them could work together in the effort to retrieve Audrey.

"Is it too late to talk to Melissa?" Russ asked.

"No, of course not, I'll get her." Answered Rachel. She got up to go get her. Russ suspected that she had already fallen asleep so it may take a while to waken her.

"Tom, I know you have been asked this a hundred times, but do you remember any of the vehicles in the parking area when you pulled in?" Tom hesitated then said.

"You know I can't recall any specifics but it seems that when I got out of the car to go to the restroom, I had to be careful not to hit the vehicle next to us with my door." Tom said. "I only remember that it was taller than the car. It had to be some kind of truck like Melissa says."

He thought for a moment. "But it wasn't there when I got back. I didn't think about it at the time, but since that night I realize that there was a vehicle there when I pulled in and it was gone when I came back from the restroom." Russ and Tom's conversation was interrupted when Rachel and Melissa appeared from upstairs.

"Here she is." Russ heard from behind and turned to see Melissa and Rachel coming around the corner from the other end of the house.

"Hello, Melissa." Russ and Tom said almost at the same time.

"She wasn't all the way asleep. She said that she wanted to meet the man that was going to find Audrey." Rachel said, looking at Russ, the implication being unintentional, but she was only being hopeful. Melissa was wearing pink pajamas with blue elephants on them. Her blonde hair was about shoulder length and her bangs kept falling into her eyes. She had obviously been asleep.

"I'm going to do my best." Russ said as Melissa sat down on the couch next to him. Russ and Melissa talked for a little while. She was able to answer a few critical questions for him. Russ was now a little more familiar with the activities that took place on the night Audrey disappeared.

"Tom, I want you to O.K. surveillance on your phone." Russ stated.

"That's fine." Tom replied. "But, why? You said that you don't believe a ransom will be involved."

"That's right, but if I'm wrong and a call does come in, we can't afford to miss it." Russ answered. "I'll call and make all the arrangements." Russ finally explained that he would be leaving the next morning to visit the scene of the crime. Russ assured them that he would maintain regular communications and he would keep them apprised of any promising information he was able to collect, as long as they abided by his guidelines concerning security. He explained the strategic reasons for the need to keep information on a need to know basis until they learned more about the circumstances surrounding Audrey's abduction.

Russ was able to keep the results of the majority of his past searches out of the conversation. The actual probability of finding their daughter safe and sound was slim, but there was a chance. Russ had developed many contacts along the way and he knew that there were two or three strong possibilities as to the purpose of Audrey's abduction. The place to begin his search was at the point of the crime and his gut feeling was that the first step from there would be in the direction of the coast, most probably the nearest harbor. The point of the crime, on I-95, was so close to the coast. Airports were too risky, boats were cheaper to operate and more difficult to track. It makes sense, the difficult part comes when you get to the water, and hopefully, there would be a trail.

"Do you mind if I call a cab?" Russ asked Tom and Rachel.

"No." Rachel exclaimed. "We have a spare bedroom and we want you to stay here tonight."

"That's very kind of you." Russ replied. "But I have some work to do and I don't want to wake you guys during the night. You need your sleep." Russ said.

Tom made the call for the cab. Rachel reluctantly acquiesced.

"O.K., but when will we see you again?" Rachel asked.

"I'll be leaving early and I'll call tomorrow afternoon, O.K." Russ answered. "You guys just stay strong for Audrey."

CHAPTER 9

Paul Rahhim picked up his phone and dialed the number of the bank in Geneva. An operator answered and Rahhim recited his account number and his personal identification code. The operator transferred him directly to the bank officer that handled his accounts. Without having to provide specific account data, Rahhim was able to transfer currency among his accounts in Geneva, the United States, Canada and the Cayman Islands. From these accounts payments would be made to the operatives that kept his operations functioning. As long as the compensation was made in a timely manner, Rahhim would not experience any labor problems. He would gladly share in the proceeds in order to keep the product flowing from their sources. A bottleneck in the cash flow would cause a bottleneck in the supply chain. This was the law of supply and demand that was not necessary to preach every morning at a sales meeting. There were few rules in this business, but the ones that do exist were vitally important. They were the difference between success and failure, which was synonymous with life and death or maybe worse, prison time.

Rahhim hung up the phone and checked his email. There were three that were junk mail and only one of any importance. Running it through the decryption software, it revealed an order from a customer that he had not heard from in a while. The message decrypted into, "Require two Caucasian females fourteen to seventeen, good to high quality." Rahhim realized that he had none of these which weren't spoken for in the pipeline at this time. His knowledge of the client and his location meant that the logical source for procurement was the west coast of the United States. He began punching on the laptop. The message he was sending would activate a chain of events that would cause someone else to lose a precious member of their family.

Two young women would seemingly disappear from the face of the earth. Rahhim knew this and it amused him that the naïve Americans would be clueless as to where their daughters had gone and that his bank accounts would be that much fatter. Even though he had accepted a western lifestyle, Rahhim still maintained a deep hatred of western culture, specifically the Godless American society. Preying on this evil culture was a natural extension of his conditioning. He felt no sorrow, no guilt. He was providing a valuable service to his clients at the expense of deserving American infidels.

*　*　*　*　*　*　*

The handgun exploded in Russell's hand. The open-iron sights had been perfectly aligned, superimposed at the center mass on the silhouette target. The nine-millimeter bullet traveled down the barrel and left the barrel at twelve hundred and fifty feet per second, transited the twenty five yards and punched a hole in the ten-ring. This shot was followed closely by five more bullets, one per second, creating a pattern only three inches in diameter measured from any angle. Accuracy at this level was difficult to learn and to maintain. Many rounds of ammunition had been expended in order to produce the level of confidence Russ Stone had in his marksmanship skills. In the lane next to Stone, Captain Wilson of the Walterboro Sheriffs Department was emptying his forty caliber rounds into his target but not as effectively as Stone had. The men flipped the switch on the partition that activated the motor, which in turn wound the cable around a wheel that returned the freshly shot targets back to their positions.

"Being promoted wreaks havoc on your marksmanship skills," mumbled Wilson. "I used to be able to hold the same pattern as you, Russ."

"You've got to get out of the office more, Stan." Russ said, trying not to sound cocky. "I shoot four days a week unless I'm on a case. You know you've got to use it or you lose it." Russ said.

"They don't authorize but one thousand rounds a year for officers in this department. The patrolmen get three times that and justifiably so," said Wilson. "I hate having to go to funerals of good men who should not have been killed."

"You're right," said Russ. "Those guys have to be on their toes twenty-four seven. You never know where the one with your name on it will come from." The two men were silent for a moment contemplating the hazards of the careers they had chosen. Russ had lost several good friends along the way and he promised himself that he would not be taken down due to lack of training or self-discipline. His skills would be maintained as long as he was in the business and when they could not be, for whatever reason, he would retire. He just hoped that he would be able to objectively critique his skills as he aged and not delude himself into thinking that the time to retire had not come when it actually had.

A mans got to know his limitations. A line from a movie he has remembered since he saw it. A Dirty Harry movie, he could even remember Clint Eastwood's snarling face as he said it.

The whine of the motor taking Stan's target back down the lane brought Russ' thoughts back to the present. He installed another target onto the holder and ran it back down to the twenty-five yard line, inserted a loaded magazine into his Smith and Wesson and punched fourteen more holes in the ten-ring. The range time was therapeutic for Russ Stone. The silence between shots was occupied only by intense concentration on the task of executing the skills needed to allow the weapon to fire while holding the sight picture to as little wobble as possible. Thus, the secret to accuracy, he had learned long ago. Squeeze the trigger and allow the weapon to fire within the smallest amount of wobble possible. Any other method could create varying amounts of trigger pressure, which will move the barrel out of alignment at the instant the firing pin indents the primer, igniting the powder. It is easy to understand such a sequence of events intellectually, but it is quite another to have the complete cooperation of all of the muscles and nerves involved. Practice was the only means by which to maintain proficiency in any physical activity requiring the organization of mental and physical skills, as any golfer with a handicap less than ten would tell you.

The two men eventually disposed of two hundred rounds a piece. They collected their gear and retired to the cleaning room where they disassembled the weapons and gave them a thorough cleaning.

"It's going to be tough finding that little girl." Wilson finally admitted what he'd been thinking since Stone arrived. His people did a good job from his point of view, but had come up empty handed. Not a single clue, as far as they could tell Audrey Clark had vanished into thin air. "Where will you start?" Wilson asked.

"I want to talk to your men, the ones on the scene first. I realize that everything they know is in the reports, but I just want to hear their story first-hand." Russ also had other irons in the fire that he was not willing to divulge to Captain Wilson, not that he didn't trust him, but sources he had developed over the years were sensitive and could only be tapped for his own cases. As far as anyone else was concerned Russ Stone was only a flatfoot, developing leads the old fashioned way. They finished cleaning their weapons and then reloaded them with service ammunition then returned them to their holsters.

"Time for lunch." Wilson said. "I know a great barbeque place."

"Sure." Stone said. "Let me check my email right quick and I'll be ready to go."

"Alright, just come to my office when you're done and we'll leave from there." Wilson said.

* * * * * * *

The Panamanian registered freighter Blue Star set sail from Galveston, Texas at about the same time Darby left the marina in Beaufort. Her course would take it across the Atlantic with its cargo of American grain. The Blue Star was a clean and well maintained vessel originally built in the northern German port of Bremen. She was sold new ten years prior to a shipping concern based in Paris. She had continued in operation under the control of the original purchaser since then. She has had only two captains. The first retired after training his replacement, and the current captain had been his first mate for six years. The Blue Star was a regular visitor to the gulf coast of the United States, where it would load grain grown in the American heartland and transit the Atlantic headed for various ports of Europe, North Africa and the Middle East. This particular trip began with a loading of wheat at Galveston. The Blue Star would make a brief refueling stop in the Bahamas before continuing across the Atlantic, passing through the Straits of Gibraltar, and then she would hug the southern coast of the Mediterranean until ultimately finding her berth at Bur Sa'id. Port said, the name most Americans would be likely to recognize, was situated on the northern entrance to the Suez Canal. From this busy port, coastal freighters could transfer smaller amounts of cargo to any location along the Mediterranean coast. The freighters stop in the Bahamas was officially listed as a refueling stop although the stop was unnecessary in terms of actual fuel requirements. It was done on each transit from the gulf coast to the Mediterranean so that a pattern was established over time. The true purpose of the stop was to maintain a regular schedule of availability to one of the freight lines regular customers. The cargo to be picked up was very profitable in that it requires relatively little space and its weight was efficient relative to the space it required. The cargo required very little maintenance in route, no refrigeration, it can tolerate any humidity, and all that was needed was regular feeding and one crewman on guard.

* * * * * * *

The Blue Star's movements in the Gulf and out into the Caribbean Sea were monitored by several agencies of the United States armed forces. All commercial vessels displacing over a minimum tonnage must file its itinerary with the U.S. Coast Guard. Any deviation from the itinerary would initiate an investigation by the Coast Guard. The strict rules on the movement of shipping in this area of the world are of course an attempt by the United States government to stem the flow of illegal drugs from South America into the U.S. and Canada. And since the events of 9/11, detection of terrorist activity is a high priority. The DEA is the ultimate authority in the control of drug flow and it has assets of the U.S. Navy and Coast Guard at its disposal. The U.S. Navy closely monitors activity in these waters as it pursues its mission of defending the free world from any and all aggressors. Nothing moves in the Gulf of Mexico and the Caribbean that isn't immediately reflected on computer monitors in several onshore facilities and no fewer than twenty of America's finest warships and intelligence gathering aircraft. Signals Intelligence assets of the National Security Agency are tasked to monitor communications of all vessels in these waters also. This intelligence source is usually the most cost-effective method of determining the intentions of the operators of the ships and aircraft in the Gulf. If one listens intently to the electronic signals emanating from the vessels, sometimes they will just tell you what they are up to.

As the Blue Star made its way toward its stop in the Bahamas, Russ Stone sipped his morning coffee and finished his bagel and cream cheese. The accommodations available in the Walterboro area were limited. Hotels of the larger towns provided a full breakfast buffet as opposed to the continental breakfast served in the smaller ones. Competition did tend to force a higher level of customer service. It was a shame that it took the threat of loss of revenue to cause some concerns to offer the quality of service that it could otherwise provide.

"Well, at least the room was fairly clean." Russ thought with resignation. He had spent the previous day talking with all of Captain Wilson's personnel who had dealt with the kidnapping. Unfortunately, there did not seem to be much more to go on. Either the kidnappers were extremely good or, more likely in Russ' opinion, extremely lucky. He was convinced that there were at least two kidnappers due to the speed at which the action was carried out, considering the fact that the younger sister and the mother had been neutralized. The getaway vehicle surely had to be parked beside the Clarks sedan to minimize the amount of time the kidnappers were exposed outside of the vehicle with the little girl.

But the result of the action taken by the kidnappers that rainy night in the reststop, and the taking of Audrey Clark against her will was where Russ must begin his search. If she was to be found it would probably require a dose of the luck experienced by her kidnappers. Russ finished his breakfast and checked out of the motel. He located his rental car in the parking lot, threw his bags in the back seat and headed toward the sheriff's department. The morning traffic was much lighter than he was used to, one of the few advantages of living in a small town. Arriving at the sheriffs department at shift change, he was accosted by the type of chaos he experienced in his own hometown. Making his way to the briefing room he began to scour maps displayed along the walls. Glancing at documents that he had retrieved from his briefcase he compared the information to the locations on the maps. He had received a compilation of all transportation facilities within a three hundred mile radius and a list of all known activity for forty-eight hours prior and seventy-two after the kidnapping. Russ would have to depend on his experience and "gut feelings" in this case, far more than he was comfortable. There were a couple destinations that were statistically higher in probability than others were. He was afraid that playing the odds was not in the Clarks favor, but that was really all that he had at this point. He made a few notes on a legal pad and then obtained several maps from the department resource office.

After finding an empty office with a desk in it, he extracted his laptop from the briefcase and plugged it into the data port on the wall.

Several emails awaited him. One in particular caught his attention. William had initiated special tasking to DEA and NSA in support of Russ' investigation. This process was really just a matter of requesting a specific set of parameters be extracted from a database that was continually updated with new information. This particular result produced several interesting movements of ships and aircraft in the days following the kidnapping. It was assumed that the victim would be moved quickly and quietly in the direction of the final destination to reduce the risk of detection. There was so much traffic in this area of the world that the logistics involved limited the authorities' ability to inspect all ships or aircraft. Again, Stone must concentrate his search on targets with a high probability for success. He made more notes on the legal pad and was startled when Wilson suddenly slapped him on the shoulder.

"Damn." Stone muttered as Wilson grinned, obviously proud of his sneaking abilities. "You don't want me to lock-up right here in your squad room do you?" Stone said catching his breath.

"Relax man; we got a couple of ex-EMT's around here. They'll be glad to pound on your chest and they won't charge you much either." Wilson said. Stone realized that Wilson must be a morning person. "You getting anywhere?"

"Don't know." Stone answered, finally back to normal. "I do have some things to look at a little closer."

"I hope we have been a little help." Wilson said with genuine sincerity.

"You guys have been better than most departments and I appreciate it. I will keep you up-to-date."

"I wish you would. The Clarks are good people. I really hate to see something like this happen to good people."

"I agree." Stone said. "I was just about to head out when you tried to kill me. Again, I appreciate your help and keep your eyes and ears open for the Clarks, O.K."

"Will do. Good luck." Wilson said as Stone packed his stuff and headed for the door. "And be careful." Wilson added, knowing that Stone had the propensity for digging deep, a habit that can piss people off, especially the kind of people he was likely to encounter on this case.

CHAPTER 10

The My Marie sat at the dock on Great Abaco waiting to be reloaded for its return trip to the coast of the United States. Her fenders protected her from the scarring effects of the wooden walkway of the marina. Darby watched the docks from a window in the coffee shop above the ships store where he ate a dry sandwich and drank a strong cup of coffee that tasted like it had been brewed the day before. It was nearly six P.M. Sometime after dark he was scheduled to receive a visitor who would tell him where to go to make his pick up. This was the only part of the trip that made Darby nervous. The people he dealt with in the Bahamas did not have their ducks in a row. Every time he came over there he decided that it would be the last time he dealt with them. He shouldn't have to dock his boat but once. But invariably, they would tell him to go to another marina or to a private dock somewhere to make the pick-up. This irregular activity of My Marie only increased the possibility that someone would get suspicious of her movements. Darby watched as the sun approached the horizon. He finished the sandwich and coffee, left enough money for the meal and a tip and headed back to his boat. Walking quickly across the parking lot and onto the dock, Darby scanned the area around the marina, he saw no one. He was walking down the dock toward My Marie when he was startled by a figure on the dock just past the boat. Darby walked on as if he hadn't seen anything. As Darby began to step onto My Marie the figure moved toward him. The figure became clearer as it exited the shadows. Darby could finally tell that it was a man, obviously a local, so he became more cautious. He stopped before stepping onto the deck and regained his balance and looked directly at the man as he approached. As the man moved into the light provided by the small lamps above the dock Darby saw his face. He remembered the man, but not the name.

"You looking for someone?" Darby asked tentatively.

"Yea, I believe I'm looking for you," the man said with an accent typical of the islands. Darby recognized the voice, but he kept that fact to himself.

"You looking for Carlos, yes?" the man asked.

"Yea, you know I am. Where is he?" asked Darby getting frustrated.

"He said for you to wait here, we will make the delivery here, O.K.," the man said quietly.

"Whatever." Darby replied, hiding his concern. He was thankful that they did not want him to move to another location for the loading.

"O.K., we be back soon," the man said, and then he walked up the dock into the darkness. Darby watched him leave and then stepped onto My Marie. He turned and sat on the bow and watched in the direction the man had gone. After a few minutes he saw the lights of a car come on as it was started. The car pulled out of the parking lot and disappeared into the darkness. Darby leaned back against the cabin and relaxed. He had no idea how long it would be before they would return. The view to the left of the marina parking lot offered an excellent vantage for watching the sunset and the sun was about to drop below the hills in the west. He decided to sit there and watch the sunset. The colors began to explode into streaks of red, yellow and orange.

This is the best part of the day. Darby thought. The colors swirled and changed as if at his command. The horizon sat waiting for the celebration to fall below it as if it hungered for the heat of the sun. Suddenly the explosion of colors disappeared. The distant hills seemed to absorb the brilliance. Darkness and silence assumed dominance over Darby's world. The feeling of peace was overwhelming. The subtle rise and fall of the deck was soothing. He sensed the familiar feelings of Sunday dinner at his mother's home. He was happy, glad to be among friends and family. A feeling of safety had soon overtaken him. He was comfortable in these surroundings, nothing to hide from, and nothing to fear. His peaceful state was suddenly ended as he watched what seemed like a hand reach into his chest and squeeze his heart. He was dragged by this phenomenon back to a place he did not want to return to.

"Hey man, wake up." Darby finally heard through the fog of sleep. Turning to the direction of the voice, Darby saw the same man from the dock standing in a small boat beside My Marie. Unsure of his current state of wakefulness, Darby rubbed his eyes and looked again to verify his first impression. Confirming the existence of the small boat, he slowly came to his feet and walked back to the stern.

Looking down into the smaller boat, Darby noticed five or six duffel bags and another man at the stern operating the small outboard motor. Darby automatically reached down to grab a duffel bag as it was being handed up to him. Finally realizing that he is loading contraband, Darby glanced around the dock to see if they were being observed. Believing that all was clear, he reached for another bag. Within a minute or so, all bags were transferred into the My Marie. Darby moved them one by one into the same cabin that the previous cargo had occupied. The forward cabin had been transformed back into its original condition by removing the shackles and chains and replacing the bed and furniture. Along the walls, the storage cabinets were replaced to conceal the mounting hardware for the chains. My Marie looked like any typical charter fishing boat now, with the exception of the duffel bags. There was really no need to try to hide them any better because if she was boarded for inspection the bags would be found anyway. The Coast Guard was thorough in its duties if suspicion was high enough to warrant an inspection. Darby laid the bags along side the bed, covered them with blankets and went topside. The small boat had left. Scanning the marina, Darby was comfortable that all was well. He checked the lines and fenders before heading to the forward berth to get some sleep. Tomorrow's trip would be the longest leg of the journey.

* * * * * * *

Audrey's aching muscles and bones had replaced the intense sadness she had been feeling. Hunger was a constant companion. The new conditions were worse than those on the first boat. Audrey assumed she was on a second boat. She could feel the movement of the ocean through the skeleton of steel surrounding her. The transfer from the first boat had been quick. She remembered being picked up and placed in a car or truck and driving for only a few minutes before being carried and thrown, literally into the cold, damp cell she now occupied. Her blindfold had been removed, but her regained vision was useless in the cramped and dark, closet size room she now found herself in. She had lost any concept of time. There were no more days or nights. She did not know how long it had been since she was removed from the comfort of her family car.

She thought about her mother, but the details of her face were becoming less clear. Why has this happened to me? She wondered. No one had spoken to her with the exception of angry commands now and then. She was accustomed to her parents explaining everything to her. If she had a question, she was supposed to be able to get the answer. But, now her situation was a complete mystery. She began to cry.

Soon, the sound of her sobbing was drowned by a rumbling, which had grown in volume over the past few minutes. Audrey raised her face from her hands and listened. Her attention now focused on the unfamiliar sounds of machinery. The hum of the engines she decided. The boat was moving. She could feel the inertia as the boat was moved away from its berth and out into the ocean on course for its next port of call. Audrey knew that the movement of the boat was taking her further away from her home. She wondered why her father hadn't saved her yet. She remembered him telling her that he would not let anything bad happen to her because he loved her so much. Audrey was hungry and cold. She dropped her head into her hands and sobbed.

* * * * * * *

The sun had fallen below the horizon and darkness had enveloped the small town on the edge of the California desert. Penny Rodriguez was enjoying her newfound freedom. She had only been driving for five weeks now. Getting her drivers license provided her an emotional lift. Most of her friends had been driving for several months. Penny was a little younger than her friends, although she was obviously prettier and smarter than they were. She performed in the top two percent of her class. Her parents were so proud of her that they gave her a new car the day she passed her driving test. The little red sports car complimented Penny's personality and youthful vitality. She was singing along with her favorite CD when she pulled into the parking lot of the supermarket. On a mission to collect a few items her mother needed to complete dinner, Penny exited her car and pushed the lock button on the remote. She heard the click of the door locks and headed into the store. On the opposite side of the parking lot sat a vehicle containing three men who had watched the activity of all who had visited the shopping center since the sun had gone down. The vehicles' engine started and began to move slowly around the perimeter of the lot. Eventually it came to a stop beside the drivers door of Penny's little red sports car and waited.

* * * * * * *

The small airstrip was not much more than a field that had been graded and smoothed so that small aircraft could land without destroying its landing gear. There was one hanger and a small administration building, which would house the operations center. This was the first stop on Russ' mission to learn more about the movements of several aircraft and ocean vessels that had departed the area shortly after Audrey's abduction. The likelihood of someone witnessing anything unusual out here in the boondocks was slim, but he had to pay attention to all of the details, for Audrey's sake. Russ questioned a tired old airplane mechanic and a secretary in the operations center. He attempted to verify the activity of two aircraft that had left this field within six hours of the abduction, but the memories of the mechanic and secretary weren't very helpful. Russ returned to his rental car and checked his maps to verify the route to one more airfield, which was on the way to the first marina on his list. He determined the route and pulled out of the gravel road onto the paved one in the direction of the next airfield. Twenty or thirty minutes to this airstrip, ask his questions, and then it would be lunchtime. He was already feeling the hunger pangs. The hotel breakfast didn't last as long as he had hoped. Russ scanned the highway for any clue to the location of a restaurant that would not poison him as he headed to the second airfield. Fifteen miles after experiencing his first tinge of hunger he found a Cracker Barrel on I-95. As he pulled off the interstate and onto the frontage road, the cell phone began singing the special little tune he programmed it to emit. He pushed the send button and placed the phone to his ear.

"Yea." Russ said into the phone.

"Russ." The voice on the other end said.

"Yea, Bill." Russ recognizes the voice of his old friend. "How is it going?"

"O.K., I guess, found a few more possible ship movements. Emailed'em to ya." Bill said.

"Good, I'll download as soon as I stop. I'm surprised that there is a cell tower around here." Russ said with a tone of sarcasm.

"In the boonies, huh?"

"Yea, but I did manage to find a little civilization in the form of a Cracker Barrel. Got to buy some stock in them." Russ said realizing that such a long sentence might not make it to Bill without dropping half way through. But Bill's response indicated that he had heard it all. They said their goodbyes as Russ pulled into the parking lot of the restaurant.

There were a number of cars there but not as crowded as it could be. Russ opened his laptop and plugged the cell phone into the USB port and dialed his server. Within a few minutes he had downloaded all of his encrypted email and scanned them for highlights. Needing food, he headed for the restaurant while digesting the info he had received from Bill.

There were several possibilities that may payoff. At least he had some leads. Most cases had few if any at all. Special software created during the digital revolution had provided law enforcement valuable tools for tracking movement of suspicious people. The system used the movements of all modes of transportation such as ships, airplanes, trains and busses to compile the database. The times of arrival, departure and destinations of every possible mode of transport in the world were filed away in the huge database maintained at a nondescript office in Langley, Virginia. If all available data was entered correctly, timeliness and routes could be simulated that show any possible movement of anything, animate or inanimate from its source to its ultimate destination. The resulting possible trails could be numerous. But a few would appear to be more plausible than others.

Once the computers had done their work, a human must make the decision on which potential route to follow. The data Bill sent had given Russ more possibilities to chew on. Three of them seemed more likely to him. They fit with his initial feelings as to the route kidnappers would have taken out of the area of Audrey's abduction. He decided to follow the one that would have provided the most anonymity along with the most efficient way to move a human out of the country. If only all the ships and aircraft could be inspected that were suspect. Russ fantasized. But he understood the reality that there was just not the manpower to do such a thing. It would take the effort of only one man if Audrey was to be reunited with the family that loves her. Russ understood that and accepted the responsibility. He finished his lunch and headed for the rental car.

Russ had just started the engine when his cell phone rang. He pushed the send button and held it to his ear.

"Hello" he said, he hadn't recognized the calling number displayed on the phone.

"Hello, Russ. This is Wilson."

"Oh, hey, what's up?" Russ said realizing who it was.

"Shortly after you left the other day we got a tip on the possible vehicle used in the Clark case." Wilson said.

"Do you have the suspects?" Russ asked feeling a break had finally came.

"We questioned them, went through the van and searched the house." Wilson answered. "We also have a dozen or so low-lifes at a bar that say the two suspects had been at the bar during the time of the abduction. So we had to release them, no evidence."

"How did you get the lead on these guys?" Russ asked.

"A man from New Jersey heard the Amber Alert a couple of hours after leaving the rest stop where Audrey was taken. He called after he got home to Jersey and asked about the details of the case." Wilson continued. "He said he saw unusual activity around a vehicle that matched the Clarks sedan. The man was in the car business and was able to provide a pretty good description of the vehicle that was parked next to the Clarks." Wilson continued. "We ran the year and make of the van through the Highway Department computers and came up with several matches in the area. One of the names that came up was a local ex-con and his van was the closest match."

"I'm only an hour or so away," Russ said. "I'm on my way, I want to see what you have, O.K."

"Sure." Wilson said. "See you soon."

After arriving at the sheriffs department Russ Stone was given full access to the case file which included transcripts of the interrogation, photos, rap-sheets, and pictures of the two men suspected of kidnapping Audrey Clark.

"All we have is the somewhat unreliable description of the van." Wilson said standing behind Russ as he flipped through the file filing everything into memory. "Considering the weather at the time and the fact that the witness didn't get the license number, we can't do much more than we have already done."

"The van was clean?" Russ asked hoping for more information.

"Nothing." Wilson replied. "No fingerprints, no hair or fibers, not even any dirt. It looked like it had been cleaned thoroughly."

Russ closed the file and got up from his chair. He felt that these guys knew more than Wilson's people were able to get out of them.

"Thanks for the access to the file." Russ said. Wilson looked at Russ as if trying to read his mind, but he thought he already knew what Russ Stone was thinking.

"Look," Wilson began. "Guys like these are all over the place around here. Our jail stays full of them. This Brooks fellow has spent a few nights with us, and he's done hard time. Our little investigation means nothing to them. They would be just as happy if they did go back to prison, they don't care." Wilson was silent for a few seconds as if he were trying to choose his words carefully. "Russ, nobody around here cares what happens to them, especially if they were involved in the kidnapping of Audrey Clark."

Russ nodded his head as if to say no more needed to be said.

"Well thanks again for your cooperation. If anything else turns up, please let me know." Russ said as he shook Wilson's hand. "I have to get back to work. Got to find that little girl, right?"

"Right." Wilson replied as Russ turned to leave.

* * * * * * *

The house sat about one hundred yards off of the small two lane road. Russ could see that there were no lights on. He drove a little further until he came to a small logging road. He pulled down the road until the car was out of sight of the paved road. Russ exited the car and made his way through the woods toward the house. The black clothes he wore made him nearly invisible in the darkness of the woods. As he approached the house he stopped and surveyed the yard. He noticed a small garage in the back and what appeared to be the van parked behind the house. He circled the yard using the woods as cover and made his way to the garage. The door was unlocked, he entered slowly. Searching the garage he found a few tools and old boxes. The sheriff's department had searched the grounds and found nothing indicating Audrey was there. He stepped over to the work bench and saw an old rusty pair of trimming shears. He picked them up and put them in his pocket. He also found a length of small rope that he tested for strength and rolled it up and put it inside a larger pocket on his pants. He walked back to the door and looked out at the house, it was still dark. Either the two men were asleep, which seemed a little early for men like that, or they were out getting sloshed at a bar. Russ assumed the latter. He made his way over to the rear door of the house. Opening the screen door he tried the door knob. It turned. He quietly opened the door and stepped in.

There was no noise. He carefully searched the house. It was empty of people. He returned to the bedrooms and searched the dressers, closets and around the beds. Under one of the mattresses he found a revolver, a .357 magnum with six rounds in the cylinder. He put the gun in his belt at his back. Behind a door he found a thirty-six ounce baseball bat that he decided would be useful. He then went to the kitchen where he found a sturdy and fairly sharp knife with a six inch blade. He slipped that into a small pocket on his pants leg. Not knowing how long it would be before these guys returned, Russ went into the living room and sat down beside a front window on the hinge side of the front door. He checked his watch, it was ten thirty. Now he would just wait.

He had noticed from the outside of the house, there were no houses within miles. There should be no problem with anyone hearing anything coming from inside the house. Fortunately there had been no dogs. He liked dogs and he didn't like to harm them if he doesn't have to. The house was quiet. Outside he could hear an owl. The wind was calm and the sky was clear. Russ Stone was used to this kind of stake out. He had become accustomed to sitting for hours waiting for a suspect or while on duty with the Special Forces. Waiting was not a problem for him. He had learned to control his thoughts and anxiety for this specific activity.

He checked his watch, eleven twenty-five. He sat and watched out the window for another thirty minutes until he saw headlights turn into the driveway. Russ stood up between the door and the window and slipped on his black ski-mask. He watched as the car stopped, the headlights went out and two men got out of either side of the car. The two men talked as they reached the front steps and then the door. As the door opened, Russ tensed, ready for action. The first man entered, then the second man entered and closed the door. Russ swung the baseball bat and hit the second man in the solar plexus. Russ knew that a few ribs were broken. The man went down on his knees. The first man turned at the noise and Russ took a step toward him and spun and sunk the kitchen knife into the man's right thigh just above the knee. The knife was driven with such force that it had entered the femur about an inch. Russ rose and sent an elbow into the first man's jaw knocking him unconscious. The second man was still on his knees trying to breathe. Russ swung the bat again impacting the side of the man's head sending him to the floor.

* * * * * * *

Jack Brooks came to due to the searing pain of the bat being pressed into one of his broken ribs.

"Shit." Jack said wincing at the pain. He looked up at the man in black. "What the hell do you want?" he muttered. Russ pressed the bat into his chest even harder. Jack groaned as he realized his hands and legs were tied and he was sitting on the floor leaning on the couch.

"That hurts, huh." Russ said. Jack could only groan, the pain prevented him from moving and he didn't think he was able to talk either. Russ eased up on the pressure a little. "As you can probably tell, I am not the police." Russ paused as Jack looked at him but said nothing. "You will tell me what happened to the little girl that you kidnapped from the rest stop." Russ explained. "I noticed that there are no houses nearby, so no one will hear you scream."

"What girl?" Jack mumbled as blood began to bubble from his mouth. Russ raised the bat and brought it down hard on Jack's left knee crushing the kneecap. Russ waited until Jack's screams subsided.

"I have got all night." Russ said. "You have lots of bones left for me to break. And when I finish with you, I will start on your friend over here." Tony Means was still unconscious and tied up the same way beside Jack with the knife sticking out of his leg. "Tell me about the girl."

Jack looked at him with stubborn resolve. Russ lifted the bat again to take aim on the other knee. Before he swung Jack said "Wait!" Russ lowered the bat and placed it back on the broken rib but did not press it in. Jack hesitated, coughed up a little blood.

"If I tell you, will you get us help?" Jack mumbled.

"You tell me what I want to know or you will die an agonizing death." Russ said. Jack looked at him and seemed to understand that the man was telling him the truth.

"We didn't hurt her." Jack started. More blood tricked from his mouth as he talked. "We took her to a marina near Beaufort and gave her to a man with a boat."

"Good." Russ said. "You learn fast. Now who was the man and what was the name of the boat?"

"Don't know that, can't know that, its part of the rules."

"What is the name of the marina?" Russ asked.

"Uh," Jack tied to remember. "Think it was Pops Marina." Jack finally said.

"Now who was the man and the name of the boat?" Russ pressed. Jack just shook his head. Russ pressed the bat into the broken rib. Jack groaned.

"Don't know, not supposed to know." Jack said painfully.

"Who do you work for?" Russ asked keeping the pressure on the rib.

"Goddamit, I don't know." Jack said grimacing. "Everything is very secret, never met anybody, all I get is phone calls and money comes in the mail."

"What kind of boat was it?"

"Fishing boat, bout forty or fifty feet." Jack said. "You might as well kill us," Jack said with a cough and more blood. "They will kill us if they find out I talked." Russ realized that he probably had all the information that he was going to get.

"Your best bet is to tell the cops this was a drug deal gone bad." Russ said. "Maybe you'll get lucky. Or if something terrible has happened to that little girl, you may just see me again." Russ put down the bat. "I bet you're glad I didn't have to use these." Showing the shears to Jack.

"Fuck you." Jack mumbled through the bubbling blood. Russ exited though the back of the house and retraced his steps through the woods. He found his car where he left it and pulled out his map of the area. He decided on the quickest route to the marina and pointed his car in that direction.

The road to the marina was lonely. The two-lane road passed through some of the poorest communities in the country. Some of the people who live in the low country of South Carolina either do not care about the appearance of their homes or they are unable to do anything about it. The land itself was beautiful, unfortunately when people arrived, the land was not given the respect it was due. The old oak trees with the Spanish moss hanging from them lining the road were just like the art Russ had seen in galleries. Further north, around Charleston black women sat on the roadside weaving baskets. These they would sell to anyone who desired one. Each of the baskets was unique since they are made by hand. The baskets were hung from hand made lean-to's until they were sold. Many of the women wear traditional dress, even during the heat of summer. The clothes worn by the women were usually from the Gullah era and consisted of long plaid or gingham patterned dresses. They also usually wore a traditional cloth or scarf on the head, a means of combating the heat of the southern sun. These roadside basket shops had been an integral part of low country tradition as far back as the Civil War, or the War of Northern Aggression as many locals still called it. Russ' route did not take him past any of this local history. Instead Russ was forced to endure the squalor and poverty, which was so prevalent in the out of the way areas of the South.

* * * * * * *

Michelle Coleman was fifteen years old now. At least that was what she believed. It seemed like an eternity since she was taken while walking to school when she was ten years old. She and her mother lived in an apartment in Queens, New York. Her father had left them shortly before her abduction. The police had wasted valuable time by suspecting the father and not following up on other evidence that may have led to

Michelle. The little apartment her mother had found was fairly nice in a decent part of town and it was near the schools that Michelle would be attending. Her mother would walk with her on the mornings that she could. But most of the time she had to be at work before Michelle had to leave for school. On those mornings Michelle walked herself to school.

It was one of those mornings that Michelle walked between a large truck and an abandoned building. It happened so fast. Suddenly she was being held tightly around her head and her stomach. The doors slammed shut and she felt herself being tied and gagged. She felt like a seam in her world had opened up and she was dragged screaming through it into another, hateful, strange world. Before she could analyze and comprehend what had happened, she felt a sting on her leg and soon she was drifting off into a third, peaceful world.

Now Michelle spent her days doing laundry and anything else Sima told her to do. Sima was a nice lady but she spoke only a little English. She had become like a mother to Michelle. But not like a real mother, more like a strict guardian. Sima obviously took orders from someone else and her allegiance was with that person. Michelle had caught glimpses of Sima's boss but she had never even heard his name. She slept and ate in a little room off of the laundry room. The room was clean and well ventilated; the temperature was controlled in such a way that she was never too hot or too cold. Boredom was a constant problem for Michelle. She had no TV or radio, only a copy of the Koran, in English, to read and a few magazines written in an unusual language. It was difficult for her to get used to the food that was brought to her three times a day but she had learned to tolerate it, even like some of the dishes.

Michelle was slowly forgetting her other life. She had to force herself to maintain her memory of her mother and others who were important to her. She cried regularly. Sima seemed to understand what she was going through but rarely had anything comforting to say. Michelle was alone and lonely. She did not realize that she was being reconditioned. The isolation and the monotonous work were an effective means of retraining her mind. Soon, Michelle would no longer be Michelle. She would be a content, dependent servant. "Misha" was the name Michelle had been given by her captors. No one called her Michelle even the first day she arrived. They asked her name once and it must have sounded like the more locally popular Misha. It was working, sometimes she found herself calling herself Misha. Her old identity was slowly fading away and her new one was taking its place.

When the others brought down the laundry to be done she found herself imitating their behavior. She used the same simple greetings and body language of those she came in contact with. But those were few. She tried to be friendly with the guards that were ever present at the top of the stairway that lead up from her laundry room, but they just tell her to go back down. The girls that bring the laundry down were similar in age to Michelle but they were curiously silent and left quickly after depositing their loads.

Michelle had investigated as much of her surroundings as she had been allowed to. Her private prison had been designed to thoroughly seal her off from other people and any form of communication. She had considered escape but her only feasible plans required getting past the guard at the top of the stairs, but that task seemed impossible to her. If she could only get to a phone, but what number would she dial? Where was she? Could she dial her mother's or father's numbers and actually get them? She didn't know the answers to those questions. She believed that due to the methods of travel and the time it took that she must be in another country, especially since everyone around her speaks a different language. She realized that she did not know how to use a phone in another country. Her thoughts of escape logically lead to gaining access to a computer. She had her own computer when she was at home that she used to email her friends. She hadn't seen a computer in the limited amount of the house that she had been in. But she believed that there must be one somewhere, if only she could ever get to it. But again, the first step in any escape plan was to get past the guards, and that thought caused the excitement of possible freedom to wane. She knew that she couldn't get past those guards.

CHAPTER 11

Abdul al-Rahish was the owner of the estate situated outside of Damascus where Michelle was forced to provide laundry services. Al-Rahish had reached his current lofty position within Syrian society by providing a variety of services to the government of Syria and by handling certain private matters for the family of the President. He had served as military liaison to the Soviet Union prior to its demise and later as the Syrian Defense Minister. The contacts developed during those years formed the basis of the empire he now controls. Al-Rahish was the foremost contact in the Middle East for military hardware. When the military-industrial complex of the old Soviet Union found itself running out of hard currency, it was glad to have al-Rahish and others like him who could turn guns and bullets into cash.

He was not particular as to who he sold arms to, with the exception of any group that supported Israel. His hatred of that country was typical of most Arabs. The tensions between the Israelis and the Arabs are the result of thousands of years of history between the various groups of people in the Middle East. Over the centuries, the inhabitants of these mostly desert countries had divided themselves into political and religious groups, each thinking that their own beliefs and ways of life were superior to anyone else's. Intolerance of the beliefs of others was the basis for the hate the groups felt toward the others. It was not limited to the Arab-Israeli tensions. There were hatreds even within the two.

Religious sects within Islam were at constant struggle. Saddam Hussein's hatred of the Kurds in the north of Iraq was a prime example. Turkey also has its problems with the Kurds on its border with Iraq. Iran's many different sects all based on Islam and the teachings of Mohammed were usually at odds with each other. The U.S. invasions of Iraq in 1991 and 2003 and the current occupation had consolidated the various sects into at least two camps; those that support the U.S. and those that don't.

Al-Rahish's estate on the outskirts of Damascus was huge. The central house was two stories with the bottom floor being a basement dug into the desert sands of Syria. This provided natural insulation and reduced the cost of cooling the building. This basement area housed the housekeeping, including Michelle's laundry room, and mechanical systems for the rest of the building. The second floor was the living quarters. It consisted of a master suite, six guest bedrooms and two offices, one for al-Rahish and the other for his assistants. The kitchen was large enough for five chefs to work preparing food for the many business meetings hosted by al-Rahish. The living room was elegant and plush, featuring ethnic furniture and Persian rugs. The room was used to impress well-capitalized quests in an effort to close lucrative arms deals. Al-Rahish's master suite and his private, more casual den were on the opposite side of the kitchen from the more formal living and dining areas. His private den featured more rustic furnishings. Most were ethnic but a few had been gathered from other parts of the world.

As Minister of Defense, he had the opportunity to travel extensively in support of his governments diplomatic efforts. Most of the foreign pieces in his den were collected from the old Soviet Union and other countries of the Warsaw Pact. The estate included immaculate security precautions including an eight foot wall surrounding the twenty five acre compound. Outside the wall were strategically positioned motion detectors and cameras feeding data into a central security computer located inside a separate guard building beside the drive leading from the main entrance of the house to the gate. There were four smaller guard shacks at each corner of the wall, each manned on a twenty-four hour basis. Two guards manned the main guardhouse, one monitored the computer and the other was shift commander. The high state of security was a leftover from the days as Defense Minister, but it was now required due to the presence of a new facility on the compound.

When al-Rahish transformed himself from government bureaucrat into international arms dealer, he found it necessary to store certain portions of his inventory close by. These pieces were needed for the purposes of demonstration and because some of the munitions he supplied are extremely difficult to acquire and therefore were priced based on their scarcity. These hard-to-find or technologically advanced weapons required additional protection over the limited security capabilities of the contract warehouse services provided to him by a business partner in Beirut. Much of the business conducted within the walls of al-Rahish's compound was with enemies of Israel, such as Hamas, Hezbolla, Islamic jihad and the Al-Aqsa Martyrs Brigade thus the need for an appropriate degree of security.

Israel's penchant for destroying facilities it felt was detrimental to the security of its homeland was demonstrated with regularity. The destruction of the Iraqi nuclear facility in 1981 was a prime example of the deadly determination of the Israeli military to prevent attacks to its sovereignty.

Today, al-Rahish was sitting in his office contemplating the status of his primary means of fattening his bank accounts when his administrative assistant appeared at his office door.

"There is a fax for you, sir," she stated in an appropriately professional tone.

"Thank you, I'll take it." Al-Rahish replied over the top of his reading glasses. He laid down the inventory report he had been reading and took the two white sheets of paper from the assistant. She nodded slightly and turned and left. Al-Rahish ignored the cover page and turned directly to the second.

"Six packages enroute set to arrive six days from the date of this message. Signed Basari."

Al-Rahish checked his calendar, slips the two pages into the shredder beside his desk. He picked up the telephone and punched a series of numbers and waited for the answer while the shredder did its job. When the click indicated the phone had been answered, he dictated his order ignoring the salutation offered by the answerer.

"Emil, get six cells ready for occupancy." That was all Emil needed to know. The order from his superior would cause him to set in motion a series of events in preparation for the arrival of a group of people that had to be reconditioned. This was Emil's full time job, supervising the new "recruits." A complete regimen had been developed and perfected over years of successful outcomes. New "recruits" would spend six months in a special wing of the compound. Al-Rahish not only benefited from the cheap labor provided by slaves, he also prepared them for the eventual sale to others who desired the services of human slaves.

* * * * * * *

The metallic clank of the small sliding door on the wall jolted Audrey awake from a fitful sleep. She looked over at the opening and recognized that someone was holding a plate of food for her. She was still trying to make herself get up to get it when a voice from the other side of the door growled in simple English and with an accent that was unfamiliar to her.

"Well, you want it or not?" the voice said.

"Yes, please, I'm coming." Audrey said quietly. She took the plate and as the little door slid closed she said a little louder. "I need a blanket; it's cold in here. Can I have another blanket please?" All Audrey heard in response was an incoherent grumble and then the sound of footsteps getting steadily quieter. A few seconds later she heard what sounded like a large metal door slam shut. As the sound of the door reverberated around inside the metal cage she was held captive in she screamed, "Let me out of here!" and began to cry before the last word left her throat. She was terrified, cold and hungry.

She remembered that she was holding a plate of food and it felt warm in her hands. She realized that if she ate it, it would help her not feel so cold. So she sat on the cold floor and sobbed while she ate what appeared to be some type of stew with a small piece of dry bread. She really didn't care what it was as long as it tasted O.K. and it was warm. Audrey's eyes were slowly adapting to the low light level of the room she was in. She looked around as she ate. The room was very small. She guessed that it was six feet square and the ceiling was only about six feet high. She concluded that she was in a box with a door. The walls, floor and ceiling were metal and the seams were riveted, she thought. She suddenly jumped with fright when she saw a roach skitter along the wall and go under the door. She was glad it was gone, but she knew that it was in the room with her and there were probably many more where that one came from. She wondered if it was possible to escape. Audrey finished eating the food and set the bowl on the floor. She walked to the door and put her hand on it and pushed. It did not budge. She pushed a little harder, still no movement. She looked for a latch or door handle but there was nothing. She suddenly felt scared again. Audrey began to cry and walked back over to the bed and laid down and cried herself to sleep.

* * * * * * *

The docks were old and in need of repair. The marina was surrounded by marshes. A gravel drive led down from the main road. Russ stood outside the rental car and stretched. The ground was covered with round pebbles. They were probably replenished regularly as the wind and tide washed many into the water. Russ scratched his shoulder as he made his way toward the ships store. It was an older building with an ice storage box beside the front door. Opening the door Russ noticed an older fellow sitting behind the counter watching a small television. The shelves held a menagerie of goods that probably covered anything that a seaman could need. Hanging from rails on the far end of the store was a variety of clothing, primarily foul weather gear. Russ strolled over to the cooler, reached in and pulled a bottle of water from the wire rack. Turning toward the counter he could see that the fellow behind the counter was watching reruns of M.A.S.H.

"I get a kick out of that show." Russ said as he went to the counter to pay.

"Yea me too. It is about all that I watch these days. Can't take that new crap," the man replied.

"It was just a matter of time before they ran out of stuff," Russ said trying to small talk.

"Is that all for ya?" the man asked.

"Yea just a little water and a little info?" Russ asked hoping for cooperation. He knew that sometimes part of the deal in docking a boat at a marina included confidentiality. Russ hoped this fellow would make his job a little easier.

"What kind of info?" the man offers. Russ felt a little more comfortable, he seemed willing to at least listen to Russ' request.

"I'm looking for a boat that may have put in here and laid over for a couple of days. It probably would have pulled out last week." Russ said as the man rang up his water and gave him his change. The old fellow closed the register and sat back down in his rocking chair.

"What you looking for it for?" asked the man.

"Friend of mine, his wife is looking for him, they had a fight, you know." Russ said.

"Yea, I know, why don't you tell me the truth now? What'd he do?" the man said with a smile.

"You're sharp." Russ said. Then he explained about the missing little girl and finished by asking to keep that info to himself for the sake of the little girl. The man looked up and said.

"You're a good man." He reached under the counter and pulled out a worn ledger book and tossed it on the counter. "If you need any help figuring out anything, let me know." Russ thanked him and opened the book. The ledger had each arrival with date and time and the amount charged for each slip. He flipped forward to the most recent activity. Scanning entries for the last ten days he noted five arrivals and departures that fit the profile he was looking for. Russ pulled a pad and pencil out of his pocket and jotted down the data on the five boats. He handed the book back to the man and thanked him for his help.

"Hope you find her," the man said in response to Russ' appreciation.

"If we do you can feel good that you helped." Russ answered as he turned for the door.

"Yep," the man said as Russ opened the door. Russ waved as he left and made his way down to the docks. He walked over to the slips that each boat had occupied. A couple already had other boats in them. A glance around each slip revealed nothing that would further his search for Audrey. Standing on the dock, Russ looked out on the channel and the marshes that lined the waterway and wondered where she could be. The wind and the sun felt good on his face. He stood there for a time as if the answer would come to him on the wind so he could take her home to her family where she belonged. A Gull flew over and circled him expecting to be thrown some food. When no food was offered, it flew to the other end of the dock and landed. It searched around for crumbs, finding a few it went airborne again and disappeared. Russ watched the activity of the Gull and realized the similarity of his and the Gulls quest. They both had found a morsel of the object of their searches which was merely enough to help them on their way to the bigger prize, a complete meal for the Gull and Audrey for Russ. Russ reached down to his belt and released his cell phone. He punched a number and speed dialed Bill's number. As he turned to walk back to his car the phone was answered.

"It's your nickel." Bill said knowing it was Russ calling.

"Got some boats I need some info on. Can you help?" Russ implored.

"Yea, I guess, what you got?" Bill said.

"Got some names and FCC call letters, you ready to copy?"

"Yep, go ahead." Bill said as he grabbed his pen and paper. Russ read off the list he had made as he walked toward his car. When he finished, Bill read it all back to make sure he had copied the data correctly.

"I need to know where those boats are and the routes they have taken since leaving these coordinates." Russ said as he opened the door to the car and retrieved his GPS receiver from his briefcase. After turning it on and initializing the unit it revealed the coordinates of where he was standing. Russ read them to Bill and again Bill repeated them back for verification.

"Thanks." Russ said. "We need a little luck. Hope you turn up something helpful.

"I'll get right on it." Bill said and hung up the phone. Russ pressed the end button on his phone and looked back at the little ships store. He closed and locked the car and made his way back into the store. Russ had one more question for the old fellow watching MASH on the little TV.

* * * * * * *

Darby closed the door to the engine room and cursed in frustration at the amount of oil that was leaking from the valve cover on the V-8 diesel. He was not worried that the engine would stop running. As long as he added oil regularly it would keep running. Darby was more concerned that the oil may leak onto the hot exhaust system and start a fire. A fire on a boat was a serious matter, second only to punching a hole in the hull. At this time the fire was the only real possibility as the water here due south of Grand Bahama island was deep enough that running aground was not likely. Every hour or so since leaving Great Abaco, Darby had to go below to sop up the oil collecting around the cover in an effort to prevent a fire hazard. He had hoped for a peaceful return trip, but that possibility was long gone. Too bad too, because the ocean was a brilliant turquoise color and the dolphins were at the bow showing the way. He stopped by the refrigerator on the way to the helm and grabbed several beers.

He sat down behind the wheel and popped the top on a Budweiser and drank half of it before putting it in the cup holder. The cold effervescent liquid quenched the thirst he had developed in the hot engine room. He looked out the windows and marveled at the contrast. The weather was absolutely beautiful, but the situation below was a disaster in the making. He glanced at the auto-pilot and then at his chart and verified that he was on the correct course and heading and then relaxed. He put his feet up on the instrument panel and closed his eyes for a while.

The soft drum of the big diesels and the splashing of the ocean on the hull could easily bring on a peaceful sleep. But even with the auto-pilot on, a human still had to be awake at the wheel to ensure safe, uninterrupted passage on the high seas.

Darby could count on about fifty minutes of peace and calm cruising before he had to go below again, but all was not as quiet eight hundred miles northeast of his position where the Blue Star, heading in the opposite direction, was battling a fierce squall line. The freighter intersected the path of the storm southeast of Bermuda. The front had originated over the Great Lakes five days earlier, the result of a blast of arctic air that had made its way across Canada. The late summer storm had brought torrential rain and several tornadoes to the mid Atlantic states. Once out over the ocean it was able to build strength by gorging itself on the warm waters of the Gulf Stream. It would eventually turn north and lose most of its strength, but in the meantime it pummeled Bermuda and the Blue Star. She was a sturdy ship. Maintenance was performed in accordance with the insurance company's specifications. As long as the crew was competent, all should be fine, at least with the ship.

In her cell, Audrey was sick. The steady rise and fall of the ship had brought on a seasickness that she had never known before. She wasn't certain why she was ill. She thought that it was maybe the food they had given her. She was mistakenly blaming the food because it was now all over the floor and she was still trying to expel it from her empty stomach. The dry heaves are a terrible feeling and quite frightening to a twelve year old girl who had never experienced them before. The ship continued to rock as Audrey thought she was dying.

* * * * * * *

In the small park outside of the office building where he worked, Tom Clark sat on a wooden bench. He watched while scores of people made their way from building to building, ate lunch or just enjoyed being outside after half a day cooped up inside a concrete tower earning their living. "What were they thinking about?" he wondered. What series of decisions had brought them all to this place at the same moment in time? Is he the only one of them carrying such a heavy burden as coping with the loss of one so dear to him? It had only been three days since Russ Stone had left their home in Atlanta and begun the search for his daughter. Time had passed so slowly, creeping agonizingly toward an uncertain ending. Russ had called every evening. He had no real information, but the knowledge that he was actually working was helpful. Tom had conditioned himself over the years to be a positive person. He expected things to turn out to his advantage. Being a career salesman, that attitude was necessary if you expect to survive in a highly competitive business world. So far Tom's mental attitude had served him well, but periodically he questioned his ability to maintain his mental stability. Sitting there now under the trees without the details of the job to occupy his mind he began to slip. Terror began to take over. Terror brought about by the real possibility that he may not ever see his beautiful daughter again. The decline got even steeper as he took the inevitable mental step that even worse than his loss, something terrible may be happening to Audrey, something horrible that she should not have to endure.

"If I could only get my hands on the son of a bitch…" Tom muttered to himself, while fighting back the tears that were forcing their way to the surface. Tom trembled with hatred for the unnamed, unidentifiable face that was responsible for the inhumane act committed on his family. "I'll kill you, you bastard, give her back, or I'll kill you." Tom muttered through an uncontrollable flow of tremors and tears as the clock ticked-away the moments of his torment.

CHAPTER 12

The information Russ requested on the boats at Pops Marina was being chewed on by the banks of computers in the I.T. center at CIA headquarters in Langley, Virginia. Russ had been able to narrow down the list of possibilities a little better this time by providing a possible starting point, the little marina outside of Beaufort, South Carolina. Audrey's rescue was still dependent on educated (if not lucky) guesses as to what route her captures had taken.

Bill reviewed the finished reports for accuracy and clarity and then uploaded them via email to Russ. The instant Bill clicked the send icon, Russ was checking into the Days Inn on the outskirts of Beaufort about six miles from Pops Marina. Russ had stopped for dinner prior to checking in. He planned to go for a run as soon as he settled in. He couldn't neglect his physical condition. Travel had a terrible effect on his bodies systems and the only way to fight the effect was to exercise.

After unpacking and changing into his running clothes, Russ took out his laptop and placed it on the desk. He plugged it into the power outlet and the data terminal and turned it on. He clicked the icon that would log onto his email server and then he left for his run. By the time he retured from his five mile run, anything that had been sent to him would be there waiting. Russ left the room, tucking the key into the small pocket in his running pants. He headed down the stairs and into the parking lot where he found a little grass to do some stretching exercises. After stretching he checked his watch and took of at a trot. He had scoped out a possible running route on his way into the motel. He should be able to confine the majority of his run in residential areas out of the way of heavier traffic on the main roads.

The going was a little tough at first due to stiff joints from sitting in airplanes and rental cars over the past few days. But he soon got into a groove and was able to maintain a healthy pace.

The neighborhoods around there were a little run down, he thought, as he made his way further from the main road. Most of the homes were clean and neat, although a little old. The residents that he noticed appeared to be retirees or younger people probably renting. Russ was forced to sidestep a pothole that appeared suddenly in his way. He thought about his wife and kids and decided to call them when he got back to the hotel. He hoped that Bill had gotten the information he needed and it would be in his email when he got back. Time was getting critical. He knew that if he was going to find Audrey he had to do it soon. His pace was good considering the state of his body. He made a left turn and ran another quarter mile through the neighborhood. Soon it would be time to turn and head back, according to his watch he was almost halfway. He made a u-turn and picked up speed. He liked to finish strong, only slowing his pace with a few hundred yards to go to cool down. He then slowed to a fast walk for the last fifty yards to complete his cool down. He stopped to walk when he got to the parking lot and then headed back to his room.

Entering the room he looked at the laptop and noticed that he had several messages. Russ went to the bathroom and grabbed a towel to dry his head and neck. He switched on the TV and sat down at the desk. Russ opened his emails and read each intently. The data took Russ about two hours to digest. He knew somewhere there was an answer. There was one piece of information that was going to be the key to unlock the secret of Audrey's location. All he had to do was keep moving the pieces around in his head. Soon the pieces would fall where they belonged and he would know. He needed no distractions, just as much information as possible to plug into the ongoing play in his head.

Russ realized that there was another piece of data out there that may help lead him in the correct direction. He made a mental note to call Bill in the morning with his request. He should have it by lunchtime. In the meantime he would make some phone calls and check a few websites that have been helpful to him in the past. He picked up his cell phone and dialed the Clarks. Rachel picked up and Russ spoke to her for a long time. The talk was therapeutic for both of them. It helped to be able to discuss thoughts about something intense as loosing a loved one. Russ was able to convince Rachel that things were progressing as well as could be expected in such a case, and then they said goodbye.

Russ got ready for bed. The news on the TV was unremarkable until he heard the mention of a missing girl. He focused his attention on the report. The girl had gone missing from a shopping center in southern California. According to the report, she had gone to the store to buy groceries and was never heard from again. Local authorities were baffled. Her red sports car seemed untouched. From Russ' perspective the coincidences were unmistakable. So many cases he had worked began with the same scenario. When would it stop? he thought. He turned off the TV and got into bed. But he knew that a good night's sleep was difficult to achieve while on a case like this because he got so emotionally involved. Russ pulled the sheet and blanket around his shoulders. He hoped his weariness would overcome his anxiety to allow him to sleep. He reached over, picked up his cell phone and set it to wake him at seven in the morning. Against the odds, he fell asleep within a few minutes of closing his eyes.

As if awakening and suddenly acquiring the ability to hear a new world of sound, Russ was drawn from a dark peaceful place. Gradually he realized that his cell phone was beckoning him to wake. That had to be the hardest thing to do, extract his warm body into the cool air from such a warm peaceful place. "What was it about life that caused a sane person to do such a thing?" he thought. "Must be the instinct for survival," he answered himself. Our ancestors must have known that to stay asleep to far into the rising sun would put one at risk of being killed and devoured by some form of prehistoric beast. Such a vivid imagination made it easier for him to arise and begin his daily chores. Russ cursed his fertile imagination for providing such motivation and began to put on his running clothes for a morning run that he had not planned. What had he dreamed about that would make him want to run so soon after the previous evening's run? He didn't know the answer. He just followed his intuition and retraced the steps from the evening before. Maybe the conversation with Rachel Clark had given him the desire to renew his energy and his resolve to find her daughter.

After his run and shower, Russ put in a call to Bill. The request he made this time was fairly simple. He needed the missing person's activity for the entire east coast over the past thirty days. Thirty minutes later Russ was able to download the data. He also downloaded two maps containing the positions of the one suspicious boat. He looked at the locations of the missing persons and then his mind returned to the little marina near Beaufort and his conversation with the old man who loved M.A.S.H.

"I wonder where My Marie is right now," he said with a bit of confidence. Russ picked up the phone and dialed Bill's number.

"Bill," Russ said into the mouthpiece with a tone of urgency.

"Yea, Russ, was that not what you wanted?" Bill replied, concerned that Russ was calling back so soon.

"No man, the reports are perfect. I believe I have a possibility. I need you to pinpoint offshore charter vessel My Marie."

"You think she's the one?" Bill asked, amazed at Russ' ability to figure things out.

"I don't know. It depends on whether she has been handed off to another boat." Russ explained. "But if she was on My Marie, with any luck, we should be able to find out who or what she was handed off to."

"If you'll hang on for a second, I'll see if I can pull up her location." Russ could hear Bill pecking on the keyboard over the phone line.

"I'll need a Coast Guard cutter to allow me to ride along to the boat's location." Russ said while Bill accessed the data base. "We need to go over that boat with a fine tooth comb."

"O.K., she's south-southwest of Grand Bahama heading west." Bill said. "It appears she made two stops in the Bahamas and now is headed back to the Florida coast."

"Where do I need to get on a cutter?" Russ asked, slightly impatient.

"Ft. Pierce. I'll call ahead and make the arrangements for you." Bill said.

Russ felt a surge of energy as he stuffed his things into his bag. He was only a few miles away from the Beaufort Airport, which was also the location of the Marine Corp Air Station. He should be able to charter a corporate jet, if not it shouldn't be too difficult to get a Marine pilot to take a training flight to Ft. Pierce.

There were no jets available for charter at the civilian field, so Russ drove over to the military operations center. He parked in a visitors spot and walked into the building. He approached the operations desk and noticed two marines at their desks.

"Hello, guys." He said. The marines looked up at him. The corporal at the front desk got up and walked to the counter.

"Good morning sir," he said. "What can we do for you?" Russ Stone explained his situation to the Marine and finally asked if there were any scheduled sorties to the Ft. Pierce area. The marine looked at Stone with a critical eye and eventually turned and looked at the board hanging above the large window that faced the flight line.

"Well, we do have something scheduled for this evening." The marine said. "But you'll have to get permission from the operations officer to board that flight since you are a civilian. I can't schedule you as a passenger without his approval."

"O.K." Stone said. "Where do I find him?"

"Down the hall, last door on the right."

"Thanks." Stone said as he left to follow the directions he had been given. He found the office and knocked on the doorframe as the door was already open. Inside the door was a receptionist. She looked at Stone and smiled.

"Come in," she said. Stone stepped into the office and introduced himself.

"Could I possibly speak to the operations officer?" he asked. She looked at him curiously.

"And what can I tell him is your business?" she asked.

"I am in need of a ride to Ft. Pierce, Florida," Stone said. "and I need his approval to board a flight."

"O.K., hang on just a minute." She got up and stepped into another office. After a few seconds she returned and motioned for Stone to go into the office. Russ stepped over to the door and entered the office. The man sitting behind the desk was massive. He made the desk look like a piece of children's furniture. As Stone approached the officer stood up. Stone looked him in the eyes, but continually had to raise his gaze as the man continued to rise. He stuck out his huge hand and introduced himself.

"Colonel Billy Stoudenmire," he boomed. Stone considered not asking this man for permission to fly in case of the possibility of making him angry. Stone took his hand to shake it. The colonel's hand engulfed his, but it was still only a firm grip although Stone was sure that he could break every bone in his hand if he wanted to.

"Russell Stone." He said looking into the huge man's eyes; he found them to be kind, confident eyes. The colonel wore a standard issue marine haircut. But the ribbons on his uniform were not standard. This man had not been a desk jockey long. He had seen action and it appeared he had seen a lot. Stone then noticed the smile. Immediately, he felt comfortable.

"Sit down Mr. Stone and tell me what I can do for you," the big marine said. Stone sat in the chair in front of the desk as the colonel sat also.

"Well' sir," Stone began. "I am tracking a kidnapped girl and I need to get to Ft. Pierce as quickly as possible and I was hoping that you guys would help me get there." The colonel stared at Stone as he spoke as if he were trying to divine the truth.

"You're not military are you?" the colonel asked.

"No sir." Stone answered. "I was Special Forces. I was in the Gulf in ninety-one, a squad leader. I left the Army for the FBI where I worked in missing persons and hostage rescue." Stone continued. "Now I am on my own but I still do a lot of work with the FBI." Stone concluded.

"I was in the Gulf in ninety-one also." The colonel began. That's why I'm flying this desk now. Had my Harrier blown out from under me and ruined my back in the ejection." They smiled, both remembering the time they spent in the desert.

"Sorry to hear that, sir," Stone said. "But frankly sir, I find it difficult to believe that you could fit in a Harrier." The colonel laughed.

"Waivers," he said. "My entire career I flew on waivers. crew chief hated me. Seats, restraints, pedals all had to be modified." The big man shook his head and laughed. "Hell, if I hadn't kept everyone stocked up on liquor, I would have been behind this desk much sooner."

"Whatever it takes to get the job done, right?" Stone said. The colonel rubbed his chin with his huge hand.

"When do you need to be in Ft. Pierce, son?" he asked.

"ASAP." There is a boat west of Grand Bahama we have to intercept." Stone continued. "They are setting me up with a Coast Guard cutter as we speak."

"Follow me." The big man got up and walked out the door. Stone followed him down the hall and into the aircrew briefing room. Several pilots were milling about or filling out flight plans. Colonel Stoudenmire walked over to an Air Force pilot who was sitting in a chair, rocking back and forth on the back two legs watching VH1 on the television. George Thurogood was belting out "Bad to the Bone" and the Air Force pilot was singing along, oblivious to anything going on around him. Colonel Stoudenmire looked at Stone with a smirk as he picked up the remote and clicked off the TV.

"Hey," the pilot yelled as he turned and suddenly saw the colonel. The pilot stood quickly. "Sorry sir," the pilot said humbly. "I thought you were one of these other yahoos around here."

'That's alright, Captain Brisendine, I understand," the colonel said. "When are you heading south?"

"Actually," the captain hesitated. "Sir, I was going to leave right after Mr. Thurogood finished that song."

"Well, it looks like the song is over doesn't it."

"Yes Sir," Captain Brisendine said resigned to the fact that he would only hear half of "Bad to the Bone."

"Good," the colonel said. "You have an extra seat, could you take on a passenger?" The captain looked over at Stone.

"Sure, where to?"

"Ft. Pierce," the colonel answered. "Russ Stone, this is Captain Bill Brisendine, call sign, The Breeze," the colonel added. The two men shook hands. "Mr. Stone is on a humanitarian mission with the FBI and needs a ride so he can catch a Coast Guard boat in Ft. Pierce."

"Sure," the Breeze said. "I'm ready when you are."

"Just let me get my bags from my car." Stone said. "And colonel would you be so kind as to have my rental car returned to the closest agency?"

"Sure I think we can handle that." the colonel said. "Well I think I'll leave you two then. Good luck Mr. Stone."

"Thank you for your help." Stone said shaking the big mans hand.

"My pleasure, hope you find that little girl." Stoudenmire headed back to his office.

"Well, you ready to bust mach?" the Breeze said with a sly grin.

"I guess," replied Stone.

"Let's get your stuff and head out to my bird."

CHAPTER 13

The weather was calm at the Coast Guard piers at Ft. Pierce. A late summer storm had passed through the day before and plowed away any clouds along with it leaving a clear calm sky. The Coast Guard Cutter Bluefin was sitting at its mooring while her crew and shore personnel completed minor repairs and replenishment of her supplies in preparation for her next tour of duty, patrolling off the eastern shores of Florida. Her primary mission for the past five years had been drug traffic interdiction. She was fitted with a state of the art stern launch and recovery system of the aluminum hulled diesel powered water jet boat. Her integrated bridge system includes an Electronic Chart Display System (ECDIS) that interfaced with the Coast Guard's new surface search radar.

The Bluefin was perfectly suited for her mission. Her crew was well trained, her Captain, Thomas C. Bullard made certain of that. Bullard was a twenty-two year veteran of the Coast Guard and was not looking forward to retirement. He loved the sea. When he was forced to retire by the Coast Guard, he would not be far from the sea. He hoped to convince his wife to sell the home and live onboard his sailboat. The kids were all grown and married. The two of them don't need much room now. Hopefully she would not be too difficult to convince. Standing in the pilothouse of the Bluefin, Captain Bullard was able to watch all of the activity on her deck. The loading of supplies was nearly complete. A data processing technician was in the pilothouse installing several new pieces of computer equipment and upgrading some navigational software. She should be ready to sail the following morning as scheduled.

Bullard loved his wife and hated to leave but he also needed the open sea. He tended to get cabin fever quickly on extended shore leave. The ship to shore phones' sudden tone interrupted Bullard's thoughts. He picked up the receiver.

"CG Cutter Bluefin, Captain Bullard speaking." Bullard's commanding officer was on the line and informed him of a little change in plans. A possible smuggler had been identified and the Bluefin was tasked to intercept and board the vessel. Bullard was also made aware of the possible connection with a kidnapping and that an investigator would be joining his crew. Bullard hung up the phone and turned to the technician.

"When will I be able to turn these things back on, son?"

"About forty-five minutes, sir," the tech replied.

"Good, thank you." Bullard said as he stepped over to the coffee pot. "I'm not sure that I remember how to use a paper chart anymore."

"Yes sir, I'll have them back up soon and they should be a little more dependable for you with this new equipment installed."

"Very well," replied Bullard. "I'll be on deck if you need me."

"Aye, Aye, sir," replied the tech as Bullard stepped through the door and out onto the platform leading to the stairs down to the deck. He shut the door and descended the stairs. There was nothing he could do down here, but he enjoyed all things that have to do with sailing. He watched with pride as his crew went about their tasks readying the boat for her tour. He walked over to the gangplank to go ashore when he noticed a young fellow coming around a building heading for his boat carrying a black duffel bag. The man approached Bullard and glanced at the nametag on Bullard's shirt and introduced himself.

"Russell Stone, sir." He said with a bearing that told Bullard immediately that the man is or was military. "Thank you for your cooperation and that of your crew."

"I'm Tom Bullard, and you're welcome." Bullard replied with a smile. "If you'll wait here I'll be back in a few minutes and we'll get you settled in."

"Thank you sir, I'll do that." Stone said, then took up a position next to the gangplank as the crewmen passed by carrying supplies aboard ship. The hectic energy of the men loading the gear and supplies hinted at the looming mission of the ship. Russ was impressed at the efficiency of the efforts of the men and women in preparation for putting to sea. The ship was clean. It was obviously well maintained. The crew seemed to take pride in her. She was their home on the high seas. He scanned the hull. There was no sign of rust and the paint was flawless. The Coast Guard designation number on her bow appeared to have been painted with care and precision. The crew and the ship must take care of each other so that man and machine can survive the rigors of duty on the open sea. Russ glanced up to the top of the pilothouse and noticed the wide range of antennas and radar transceivers. A Stars and Stripes flew proudly from her flagpole on top of the pilothouse. "We shouldn't be lacking for data on this trip." Stone thought. He assumed that the newness of the vessel was an indication of the technology she bore. Russ was startled by a presence behind him. He turned to see Captain Bullard.

"I hope she meets with your approval." Bullard said.

"Impressive, the ship and the crew, I'm looking forward to seeing the inside."

"Well, let's go on board, I'll take you on a tour so that you will know your way around."

Russ followed Captain Bullard up the gangway and into the door below the pilothouse. They went directly to one of the guest cabins where Russ dropped off his gear. The galley was just a few doors aft of Russ' cabin and he was glad it was so early on the tour. He was starving and there were sandwiches and snacks available. They both ate a sandwich while Bullard explained the Bluefin's capabilities and history. Russ was sincerely intrigued. He was fascinated with this type of information. He loved machinery, especially the military kind. After they finished their lunch the tour resumed with stops in the crew quarters, the engine room and finally the pilothouse. The electronics tech was gone and had obviously completed the upgrades. The electronics were in perfect order.

Bullard took advantage of Russ' tour to check out the systems, Russ was glad to oblige. The equipment was impressive. Russ was particularly impressed with the Electronic Chart Display System and the Surface Search Radar, which he suspected would be useful in locating My Marie.

"Our departure has been moved forward twenty-four hours due to your mission," stated Bullard. "We will set sail once all of the supplies are stowed and all of our crew is accounted for."

"I appreciate your understanding. I'm unsure as to whether the missing little girl is still on the boat, but if we can ascertain that she was on it, then we can track her further." Russ explained.

"We will do all we can. We should be underway in an hour or so." With that Bullard took a quick look out the window at the progress of the supplies and then picked up the phone and called the engine room to inquire as to its status. Russ stepped back and observed as Bullard prepared his boat for duty.

* * * * * * *

A well-timed northward turn had quickened its passage through the storm front. Now the BlueStar was plying calmer waters on its way to the Mediterranean. Her Captain was experienced. The squall line had been expected since leaving its mooring in Great Abaco. It was only a matter of degrees as to how much of the weather the BlueStar would be forced to endure. The big ship would skirt the eastern edge of the storm with minimal effects on its timetable.

Audrey was miserable. The bout of seasickness had drained her of all of her strength. A crewman cleaned her cell and gave her some warm wet towels and a few dry ones so she could clean herself up a little. She was able to use the towels, but with little energy and with shaking hands. She was lying on her cot covered with only the sheet and the one blanket they had given her. Audrey shivered and cried. Suddenly the door creaked open. The crewman that cleaned her cell stepped in and asked if she needed anything else. Audrey managed a weak "no" though her tears. The crewman looked at her with some concern and said "O.K., I'll check on you soon." He locked the door and left. Audrey had wanted to beg him to let her go, but she was still too sick and certainly too weak. She had never felt so terrible. She closed her eyes and tried to sleep.

* * * * * * *

Darby cursed the leaky valve cover as he used the last of his paper towels to sop up the oil around the intake manifold. He didn't risk tightening the valve cover bolts any further due to the risk off stripping the threads or further damaging the gasket. Darby tossed the oily towel in the waste container and headed up to the helm. He needed to get some miles under him before he had to go below again to clean the oil. He started the engines and throttled them up to cruising speed. He checked the way points on the navigation system and set it, and then he headed into the galley for a beer. The water was smooth and it was a beautiful day. He felt good about this trip, no real problems except for the damn oil leak. He popped the top on the brew and flipped on the stereo and then inserted a CD. He flipped the switches that allow music to feed into the helm as well as the salon. He turned the volume up to a good forceful level and assumed his normal position in the captain's chair with his feet propped up on the helm. Darby released the lever on the side of the chair that allowed the back of the chair to recline a little so he would be more comfortable. He glanced at the navigation system. Eight more hours and he'd be pulling into Jupiter Inlet, a little harbor about twenty-five miles north of West Palm to make his delivery. Once this last detail was handled, he'd be rid of anything that could put him behind bars for a very long time. Then and only then can he motor back up to Murrells Inlet with a certain peace of mind and a fatter bank account.

He checked the navigation system again and then his radar. Everything was clear so he laid back and closed his eyes. Hopefully he could catch a few winks before he had to go back and clean the oil of the engine. The pitch and roll of the boat was soothing. The hum of the powerful engines was constant under the volume of the music playing on the stereo. Darby drifted off into a peaceful sleep. The variety of sounds melded into a hum that he had grown accustom to. For a few minutes Darby fluctuated between minimal consciousness and a deep sleep.

It began subtly at first, the rhythmic sound, like a light going on and off in a distant, foggy place. The sound strengthened as he drifted closer and closer, more distinct as his awareness heightens. Darby opened his eyes, realizing that he was being summoned. He tried to focus on the source of the sound. Contact. Something was approaching. He sat up, and then stood, scanning the horizon. Yes, to the starboard, he saw in the distance. Picking up binoculars he raised them to his head. Spinning the little wheel between the eyepieces the object comes into focus. Coast Guard, he realized.

"Shit!" Darby said. He laid down the binoculars and slid down the ladder to the salon, still only slightly awake, nearly tripping over the door guide in the floor.

He ran to the master stateroom where he stowed the duffle bags. Darby dragged them into the salon. He went below to the engine compartment and grabbed two of the cinder blocks he carried for this particular situation. He tied the first two blocks to two of the duffel bags. He went below again and brought up two more and tied them to the other two. He was not certain that one cinder block would cause the bags to sink. He went below for four more blocks and extra rope and tied them to the four duffel bags also. Confident that two blocks each would cause each bag to descend below the surface and into a watery oblivion, he went forward to check on the course of the Coast Guard vessel. He stared intently at the surface radar and then out to starboard. The vessel was heading straight toward him. But there was no radio call yet. Maybe— The radio clicked, Darby froze.

"MyMarie, this is WPB87318, Do you read? MyMarie This is WPB87318 Coast Guard patrol boat BlueFin, Do you read? Over."

"Damn," Darby muttered as his heart began to race. He turned and descended the ladder to the salon without answering the call. He grabbed one duffel bag at a time and dragged them through the door and pitched them over the side, hoping the other vessel did not see him.

He repeated this three more times and then watched the last one briefly to make certain that it sunk. The water was so clear that he was able to watch as it descended into the clear blue-green water. He turned and climbed the ladder to the helm. The radio was still producing the call from the BlueFin. Darby nervously took the the mouthpiece from its clip. He pushed the button.

"Coast Guard vessel this is My Marie, over."

"My Marie this is Coast Guard patrol boat BlueFin, you are ordered to kill your engines. I repeat please kill your engine and prepare to be boarded, over."

"BlueFin This is My Marie, what is the purpose of the boarding? Over." Darby inquired. But he knew that there would be no answer to the query.

"My Marie This is BlueFin, we will explain, kill your engines, over." Darby reached over and pulled back the throttles and went dead in the water. But he did not turn off the engines. He will wait and see what happened. He knew he couldn't out run the cutter but he held out hope that something miraculous may happen that would allow him to flee.

* * * * * * *

The BlueFin had set sail four hours earlier and set a course that would intercept My Marie. They had proceeded at top speed. Russ Stone had made himself comfortable in the pilothouse at Captain Bullard's invitation. Russ was thrilled to be able to watch as the crew performed their duties with remarkable professionalism. He had been introduced to each crewman and given a description of his or her primary duties. The MyMarie's position was pinpointed on the ECDIS as soon as BlueFin left her mooring. The BlueFin maintained a data link with several global positioning satellites. My Marie's position was never in question. The navigation system automatically guided BlueFin to its ultimate interception of My Marie. As soon as BlueFin came within visual range of the My Marie a camera was trained on her. All activities onboard her were recorded and the images were monitored in real time by the intelligence facility below the pilot house. The camera caught the crew throwing something overboard and the location was noted. The runabout would be launched and the items recovered if they had not sunk to a depth below the limits of the divers that would deploy to recover them.

The first mate noted that My Marie had gone dead in the water and appeared to be ready to be boarded. The boarding crew consisted of a security detail of three men and a search team of two. The subject vessel would be secured and then searched from bow to stern. Seldom did anything slip under the noses of the professionally trained personnel of the BlueFin. She had intercepted and boarded hundreds of vessels suspected of drug smuggling and most had paid off with the seizure of millions of dollars in illegal drugs. The vessels confiscated during these seizures were eventually sold on the open market and the proceeds were used to finance drug interdiction.

Captain Bullard maneuvered the BlueFin with the efficiency of a man who understood his vessel well. He brought her beside My Marie as the security detail trained their weapons on what they believed was the only crewman aboard the My Marie. The leader of the security team barked orders to the lone crewman through a bullhorn. He had him stand with his arms out to his side as the BlueFin approached. The crewmen of the BlueFin placed fenders between the two vessels and held them together until the five men were safely aboard the My Marie. Once the transfer was complete and the crewman handcuffed and secured, the BlueFin backed off and launched the runabout with her compliment of two divers and two crewmen. The runabout fired her engine and circled the Bluefin on its way to the area where the dump had been made.

Aboard the My Marie, the search team stood by until the security team had gone over the boat to ensure there were no other crewman or passengers and that the vessel was safe for the search team to operate. In the pilothouse of the BlueFin, Russ Stone held a pair of binoculars up to his eyes and observed the progress of the operation. He watched and listened as the crewmen onboard the BlueFin guided the runabout to the approximate area of the dump and watched as the divers fell backwards into the water to hopefully retrieve some evidence.

This effort was usually fruitless because the smugglers normally added enough weight to the containers to ensure that those sank. But sometimes they were not so lucky and they did not add enough. The contraband either floated on the surface or it sank to a level where it would level off and just hover. Sometimes smugglers would use a system that would carry the contraband to the bottom. Then it would sit there for a while. A timer built into the package would cause an air bladder to inflate, bringing the package back to the surface sometime later. The contraband was then picked up by another boat, which completed the planned transaction.

Russ panned over to the fishing vessel and observed as the security detail emerged from below and gave the all clear signal and the search detail began its work. Russ zoomed in on the single crewman seated on the floor at the rear of the vessel. He appeared unremarkable to Stone. He was a fairly clean-cut. Caucasian. He appeared to be about forty years old. He appeared distressed but not argumentative. Russ was confident that the man knew something about Audrey's whereabouts. He just couldn't wait to get over to the fishing vessel and have a look around himself and to question the lone crewman. Bullard agreed to allow Stone to have some time alone with who ever they found on My Marie for the purpose of questioning and hopefully securing information that would put them a little closer to finding the missing girl.

Russ Stone would have to wait until the search detail had finished its job and the crewman of the My Marie transferred aboard the BlueFin and secured in her brig. If they could establish that Audrey had been aboard this vessel, it would mean that she had been handed off to some-one else at one of its stops. Depending on the level of security practiced by the people involved, the crewman may not know where she went. The work had just begun. Russ thought. We would be lucky to find her.

The radio crackles to life.

"Team one to BlueFin are you ready to copy?" The security team leader said.

"Copy team one," replied the first mate from his position in the pilothouse. Russ Stone and Captain Bullard listened as the team leader read the name of the captain of My Marie and other information pertinent to the investigation of the boat as a drug smuggler. The first mate typed the data into his computer terminal. "Hold one BlueFin." The security team leader said as the search team leader interrupted him. "BlueFin, our search is complete. We are ready to transfer the crewman. Over."

"Copy team one," said the first mate. Captain Bullard gave the order to close with the fishing vessel to retrieve personnel. He turned to Stone and smiled.

"She's all yours. Take as much time as you like."

"I shouldn't be long, I'm sure your men were thorough." Russ said as he turned toward the door of the pilothouse. He slid down the stairs as if he'd been on the boat for years. He stood at the starboard side waiting for the two vessels to come together. As the security team brought the handcuffed man aboard, Stone took a long look at him.

"I'll be with you in a moment." Stone said as the man passed. Stone stepped onto the My Marie and a member of the search team approached him.

"We found something unusual below." He said. "It probably has something to do with your investigation."

"What is it?" Stone asked.

"Why don't I show you?" Stone followed the team leader through the salon and down into the forward stateroom. The team leader stepped inside while Stone stood at the door. The team leader pulled on the small table that appeared to be built into the bulkhead beside the bed. Stone watched as it slid out from the bulkhead. There were brackets bolted along the bulkhead about a foot above the floor. Stone looked at them uncertain at first what it meant.

"They didn't mean anything to us either until we found this." He set the table back into its position and lifted the mattress on the bunk. Under the mattress was a door, about eight inches square. The team leader opened it and reached inside. Stone heard a clanking sound as the sailor withdrew a set of chains from the compartment. The team leader said that there were eight sets of brackets in total. The rest were behind the removable bunk.

"Damn," Russ muttered.

"Yea," the team leader said. "This guy is not just running drugs is he?"

"Son of a bitch." Russ said. "Did you find anything else unusual?"

"No, This is it, everything else seems normal."

"Thanks, you guys do good work." Russ said as he patted the team leader on the back.

"No problem," the team leader said. "I got two kids at home, a boy and a girl. I'll be glad to kick this guy's ass for you if you want."

"Thanks, but I'm saving that pleasure for myself." Russ said as he turned and headed back toward the deck. As Stone reached the salon, he glanced over to the BlueFin. She was hauling in the runabout. Captain Bullard was standing beside the ramp. He saw Stone standing on the My Marie and gave him the thumbs up indicating the divers were able to retrieve something from the water. Once the runabout was secured in its mounts, BlueFin crewmen attached a tow line to My Marie. Russ made his way to the brig to hopefully extract information from the incarcerated captain of the seized vessel. As he entered the brig he saw Darby sitting on the bunk with his back to the wall hugging his knees. Darby glanced at Stone.

"My name is Russ Stone," he began. "Can we talk?" The prisoner hesitated as if considering whether he should wait for an attorney or not. Finally he spoke.

"Yea, sure, are you DEA?" Darby mumbled, looking at the floor.

"No, I am not. What is your name?"

"Darby, Tillman Darby," he said. "I guess I'm up the creek without a paddle this time, huh."

"It looks very serious." Stone continued. "They don't take too kindly to people who continue to replenish the streets with this stuff." Stone said trying to enforce Darby's opinion of the charges he was facing. "There is also the little matter of smuggling human beings. That may cause you some trouble too." Darby looked as though he had been shot through the heart. He knew his boat would be searched but he was certain that they would not be so thorough as to find the brackets and chains.

"Shit," was all Darby could think to say as he laid his head down on his knees. Stone was hoping to increase the pressure inside Darby's head enough that he would tell him what he knew about where Audrey may be. He waited a few more seconds before continuing the questioning.

"You know, I don't give a damn about the drugs. I am here to find a little girl that I believe was part of your cargo." Darby looked up at Stone.

"What can you do for me if I cooperate?" Darby asked, his voice cracking.

Bingo, this guy is easy. Stone thought. The thought of years and years of prison being passed from one gnarly convict to another has a way of motivating one to do the right thing.

"All I can promise is to inform the authorities of your cooperation and the regret you expressed to me about the actions you have committed recently." Darby nodded his head.

"What do you need to know?"

"Was one of your cargo a little girl, twelve, her name was Audrey?"

"I don't ask names, I just picked'em up and take'em where I'm told. But there was a girl about her age, yea." Darby answered. Russ reached into his pocket and pulled out a small photograph and held it up so Darby could see it.

"Is this her?" Darby turned toward the barred door and squinted at the picture.

"That looks like her. I didn't see much of her, but that looks like her."

"Was she alright? You didn't hurt her did you?" The tone of Stones' voice told Darby that he cared about the girl and if he found out that he had hurt her he would not be very helpful in Darby's defense.

"No man, I just took her onboard. Fed her a little, she was starving when she got to me. I took good care of all of them." Darby begged. "And I didn't touch any of them, I swear."

"Where did you take her?" Stone asked.

"Great Abaco, a little marina on the northwest side."

"What did you do with her once you got there?"

"Some people picked them all up that night." Darby said. "I don't know where they went, my job was over." Darby ended with a tone of finality that told Russ that he had probably told him all that he knew.

But he pressed on anyway.

"What did they do with them when they got to the island?" Stone continued. "Do they put them on another boat? An airplane?" Darby knew nothing else so he knew he had to convince Stone of that.

"Look, this guy's security is good." Darby said. "I do my little part and then someone else takes over. I don't want to know anything else. I will probably be killed for telling you what I have. I think they even know who my family is, I am probably killing them too." Darby said, trying to control his emotions.

"This guy you mentioned, tell me about him." Stone continued. Darby told how he was recruited and the system that was used to communicate. The tone of Darby's voice revealed his acceptance of the inevitable. His life as a free man was over. He wanted to help Stone but he had no useful information other than confirming the fact that the little girl had been on his boat. Stone listened to his story as long as he would tell it in case he had any other useful information. Darby finally stopped talking. Stone felt like the man had told him everything. Now, he had more work to do. He said his farewells to Darby and headed to his cabin.

Russ stopped by the galley on his way and grabbed a cup of coffee. In his room he laid his laptop on the small desk, plugged it in and turned it on. He opened the files containing the vessel activity that Bill had sent him. Now he was able to narrow his search down to a specific time frame. Audrey could not have been transferred until Darby had arrived. So he made a short list of three possible vessels and routes. He sent an email to Bill requesting current information on the suspect vessels. He wanted Bill to get right on it, so he went to the pilothouse and requested the use of the ship-to-shore phone. Bill answered and Stone informed him of the email and asked him to put a rush on it. Russ was about to put the phone down when he decided that it might be a good time to give the Clarks an update. He dialed the number then turned and watched as the My Marie followed obediently behind the BlueFin, tugging gently at the cable attached to her bow.

* * * * * * *

Audrey was asleep in her cell as the Blue Star made her way at twenty-one knots on her course northeast toward the Straits of Gibraltar. The water was calm and the afternoon clear. Audrey was feeling better now though she still felt dirty and needed a bath badly. The sleep was a welcomed event. Her seasickness had made it impossible for her to get any rest. For the time being she was peaceful, even becoming accustom to the sound of the engines and the motion of the vessel as she plowed the waters of the Atlantic on her way to an unknown destination. Audrey managed to sink into a peaceful, much needed sleep. Her mind took advantage of the REM sleep that it had been unable to achieve for the past few days. Her brain sorted and filed and discarded the accumulated data so it would work efficiently again upon her awakening. The process of mental maintenance was necessary to keep the human mind in a healthy state of balance. Audrey had become so distressed because of her situation that she had ignored her need for rejuvenating sleep but eventually had no choice. Luckily, nothing was keeping her brain from shutting down and performing its much needed maintenance.

* * * * * * *

Russ knew that it would not take long for Bill to gather the requested data and email it to him. He left the pilot house to roam around the deck a while until enough time had passed. Then he would access the info and hopefully find his answer. The deck of the BlueFin was immaculate. Everything was in its place and painted a brilliant white, with the exception of the safety gear which was an orange color. The runabout was being cleaned and gone over by two crewmen. It seemed that no one had to be told what to do. Only infrequently did he hear an order given over the loud speaker. This was a well trained crew. The beautiful ship had a crew worthy of her. Russ checked his watch and realized that Bill had enough time to get the work done so he headed for his cabin.

Russ downloaded his email and waited. He picked up his coffee cup, which he found to be cold. He went to the galley for some fresh java. When he returned he clicked on the attachments Bill had sent. One of the possibilities, a fishing vessel was headed in the wrong direction, so was the aircraft that he suspected. They would not head back to the U.S. coastline. The third vessel was suspicious in a number of ways. The Blue Star. Why would such a large freighter stop so soon after loading at a port in the Gulf of Mexico? This was the one. Stone decided. It was of course possible that Audrey was still on the island waiting for a later means of travel, but Russ Stone did not think so. He believed that the people who were responsible for her kidnapping would want to get her to her destination as quickly as possible.

It was obvious to him that the kidnappers have a simple and efficient system for removing people from their lives and moving them toward some yet to be determined destination. Stone was convinced Audrey was aboard the Blue Star. Now the question was how to get to her? It appeared that the freighter was headed for the Mediterranean. Russ realized that he needed to get to her before she could be off-loaded at a port. He had to get to the Blue Star before she docked.

CHAPTER 14

A twenty year veteran of the FBI, Assistant Director Ben Fletcher was a tough, competent professional. Seated behind his desk his standing height of six feet three inches was concealed. Seated across from Fletcher, Bill Barnes at five feet ten, was glad to have been asked to sit down as he entered the office. Bill had done little field work during his career at the agency. His knack at gathering information and reporting it with concise efficiency helped keep him where he was most useful. He really did prefer to stay in the office and let others like Russell Stone do the legwork. Fletcher, on the other hand, was an experienced field operative. His military experience gave him the background and the interest to help form the agency's Hostage Rescue Unit. Rarely did he get to go into the field now as the FBI needed people seated at desks with pen in hand to keep the paperwork flowing in the proper direction and at the proper speed.

Fletcher disliked that aspect of his job but he understood its necessity and got it done in a timely manner. His desk was always free of paper. Anyone who visited his office was totally unaware of the amount of paperwork that actually got done by Ben Fletcher. He was in the office by six AM each working day, well before the majority of others who worked in the same building. Today was no different. He reviewed the stacks of reports left on his desk the previous afternoon and had them back on his administrative assistant's desk before she arrived for the day.

Bill Barnes was more typical of most in the agency. He arrived around eight or so today and immediately picked up the phone and dialed Fletcher's number. The appointment was for eight thirty and Bill arrived on time to find Fletcher enjoying his second cup of coffee.

"Yes, I'm sure that we will be able to assist," said Fletcher. "Where is Stone now?"

"Aboard the BlueFin with the subject vessel in tow back to Ft. Pierce." Bill replied.

"If you guys are correct, it sounds like a highly effective smuggling operation. I'm sure I'll be able to garner the support we need."

"Good." Bill replied. "By the way, Stone needs transportation to Rota, Spain." Bill had already begun making arrangements with the Navy for the support Stone would need. The back channel contacts he had developed over the years was extensive and effective.

"We'll task a jet to pick him up when he arrives at Pierce. I'll make the arrangements. I'll call you with his contact at Rota." Fletcher said while obviously contemplating the possible alternative tactics. "If we monitor the boat through to its ultimate destination and delivery points, we could possibly catch some bigger fish."

"Yes sir, but we don't know the condition of the victims and a delay in rescue could cost lives." Bill added knowing where Russ would stand on the issue. Getting Audrey out would be his primary concern. Anything else would be an added bonus. He would accept any follow-up action as long as the girl was removed from danger.

"Understood, their rescue is the priority, but we should try to shut them down if possible." Fletcher countered. "What is the location of the freighter?"

"The Blue Star," Bill was trying to refresh Fletchers memory. "is about five hundred miles southwest of Sao Miguel in the Azores steaming northeast toward the Strait of Gibraltar. She is making about eighteen knots."

"O.K., let me make some phone calls and I'll call you soon. Thank you. And good work Bill." Fletcher rose and leaned across the desk and shook Bill's hand.

"I look forward to catching these bastards." Bill said as he turned to leave.

"We will." Fletcher said confidently as he reached for his phone. Over the next hour, Fletcher made a flurry of phone calls. The first being to the director's office to inform him of the operation that was being planned in case there were any political aspects that left him unaware. His next call was to the NRO, the National Reconnaissance Office, to request special tasking for the aerial surveillance of the suspect vessel.

Then a call was placed to the Department of the Navy to request assets be assigned in support of the mission. Fletcher was successful in collecting a vast array of support including an FBI executive jet standing by at an airfield just outside Ft. Pierce to ferry Stone to Rota, Spain with appropriate haste.

* * * * * * *

Lieutenant Max O'Brien's SEAL Platoon had just finished its morning five mile run. The weather at this time of the year in Rota, Spain was incredible. O'Brien's platoon was normally located at its home station of Little Creek, Virginia. But each of the four platoons of SEAL Team Eight rotated ninety day tours at the forward area of operations at Rota. The Mediterranean was part of SEAL Team Eight's area of responsibility. The forward basing of a trained platoon gives the Pentagon more capabilities in the event of an emergency.

The late summer sun and the cool ocean breezes were refreshing and made the morning physical fitness requirements almost enjoyable. Chief Petty Officer Dan Stromyer brought the team to double time for a cool down walk before dismissing the platoon.

"The men made good time this morning." O'Brien said to his Platoon Chief.

"Yes sir, Stromyer replied. "We will give you the numbers on the tests that I promised."

"Thank you, Dan I trust you. I'll see you at the training meeting at ten hundred hours, O.K."

"Aye, Aye sir." Stromyer replied as he trotted off to shower and change into his duty uniform. The monthly physical condition test was scheduled for the following week and O'Brien wanted to be certain that his platoon had the best numbers. The King award was a competition between the eight SEAL teams around the world. The team with the best scores win the trophy for that year. The scores were collected, tallied and posted at SEAL Training Headquarters at Coronado, California. A plaque hangs on the wall of Headquarters Southern Command with the SEAL teams that win each quarter. O'Brien intends to have his platoon contribute the highest scores of Team Eight this quarter. Team Eight had not been able to claim the honor since O'Brien took command of his platoon eight months ago. The platoon was dismissed so they could complete individual tasks on the training schedule. O'Brien wished that the schedule allowed for more pool work so they could improve on their water skills, but with the addition of new tasking assigned to his team the classroom time was needed for real-world briefings.

Team Eight had been busy recently with political unrest spreading like a plague throughout the Middle East and the southern former Soviet Union states. O'Brien's platoon had completed three operations since he took over. All were successful. Chechnya had been the most difficult. Two of his platoon members had been wounded. Seven members of a western oil-drilling contractor had been taken hostage and held for ten days by a Muslim splinter group. The location of the hostages had been known from the start as the kidnappers were not very strategically competent. But they were well armed and determined. It was as if they wanted to lure a military force to their location simply for the sake of a battle. Worldwide media exposure was all that they had wanted. The number of dead was irrelevant.

As it turned out, the number of dead was limited to the twelve kidnappers. The action was carried out quickly and subtly enough not to attract the attention of the media. With the exception of a few small stories in European newspapers, there was no coverage.

O'Brien made his way down the sidewalk in front of SEAL Team Eight Headquarters and entered through the front door. His second in command, Lieutenant JG Stanley Johnson sat in his office taking care of paperwork as he drank his second or third cup of coffee. The two officers rotate daily physical training with the platoon while the other stays behind at headquarters in case a warning order was received from Naval Special Warfare Command. Otherwise the administrative personnel handled any other routine communications.

"Morning Johnson, what's shaken?" O'Brien asked as he entered his office across the room from Johnson's.

"Same old stuff. How was our time this morning?"

"Good, the men are looking forward to putting some good numbers on the board, I believe," replied O'Brien enthusiastically. O'Brien's office was spartan, with only a few pieces of paper on his desk and a picture of his wife on the corner. Since they are only in Spain for ninety days there was no need to bring anything but essentials. The office and the barracks would be manned by another platoon from SEAL Team Eight in sixty-three days anyway. "Is everything ready at the armory for weapons maintenance this afternoon?" O'Brien asked.

"Yes sir, I spoke with Townsend a few minutes ago. He will have his armorer there and the armory open at thirteen hundred hours," replied Johnson. "If there is a problem this time, I'll throttle Townsend myself."

"As long as I get to watch." O'Brien Said with a smile. He sat down and picked up the declassified intelligence reports that were placed on his desk every morning. There was nothing unusual in the reports so he decided to head to his room, shower and change into his duty uniform.

* * * * * * *

As Russell Stone's jet was making its final approach into the airfield at Rota, the Warning Order was transmitted from the Naval Special Warfare Command to the secure communications facility located about a mile from the SEAL barracks. As he stepped into the cool late summer air an admin specialist was knocking on Lt. O'Brien's door. He opened the door with only a towel around his waist to see the young seaman standing there with his eyes wide with a hint of fear or maybe simply nervousness.

"Sir, Lt. Johnson sent me to get you. Something about a warning order. The nervous seaman muttered. O'Brien understood the Seaman's' mental state as he was newly assigned to the unit and was only three months out of his technical training.

"O.K., tell him I'll be right there," the seaman turned and hurried back up the hallway as O'Brien closed the door to finish dressing. He knew Johnson would be handling the Order with the proper amount of competence. He did not have to worry about that. What he did not know was that the Order required a recall of all members of the platoon and deployment twenty-four hours hence.

A car with General Services Administration markings was parked beside the operations building. The driver had been instructed to pick up a passenger named Stone and drive him immediately to the SEAL Team Headquarters. Stone approached the driver who was standing beside the front of the car and asked if he was his transportation.

"If you are…." he hesitated and looked down at the form in his hand. "Mr. Stone, then yes sir this is your ride."

"Yep, I'm Stone, I believe we are supposed to go to the SEAL detachment, is that correct?"

"Yes sir, that's what it says here. Can I help you with your bags?" the driver asked as he moved toward Stone.

"No, I've got them, thanks." Stone said as he placed the bags into the back seat. Ten minutes later Stone found himself standing outside of a tan building with a three by five sign in front that identified the building as the SEAL headquarters. He thanked the driver, grabbed his bags and entered the building. As he entered a nervous seaman got up from his desk and introduced himself and asked if he could help him.

"Just point out Lt. O'Brien for me please." Stone said.

"Yes sir, he should be back in a moment, can Lt. Johnson help you, he is the assistant platoon leader?"

"Yes, that should be fine. Thank you." Stone said as he set his bags on the floor. The Seaman turned and knocked on the doorframe of the office to Stones left.

"There is a gentleman here to see Lt. O'Brien, can you help him?"

"Sure." The voice from inside the office said. A second later Lt. Johnson emerged from the office.

"Hello, I'm Lt. Stan Johnson," he said extending his hand toward Stone.

"Russell Stone," he said. "How are you doing today?"

"Fine, welcome aboard. Lt. O'Brien is at the operations center. He is expecting you. Is there anything I can do for you until he gets back?"

"Well, I was hoping to get a room here with you guys, is that possible?"

"Sure." Johnson turned toward the admin specialist. "Seaman, make a room ready for Mr. Stone. Get linens and towels from the supply room and bring the key back to me."

"Aye, Aye sir," replied the Seaman as he hurried off to carry out the orders he had just been given.

"Why don't you come into my office and have a seat while he takes care of your room? Would you like a cup of coffee?" Johnson asked.

"No, thank you." Stone said as he entered the lieutenants' office and took one of the two chairs in front of the desk. Lt. Johnson walked around and sat behind the desk.

"I only got a little of the info regarding this Warning Order before O'Brien headed over to operations." Johnson said. "It's a little unusual to have someone working so closely with us on something like this."

"I'm sorry about that." Stone said. "I'm sure that having someone like me along that you are not sure of makes you a little nervous. But I assure you that I am fully qualified and I will not get in your way." Stone continued. "My interest is in the hostage only." Stone said trying to reassure the lieutenant. Johnson was about to say something when a call came in. A seaman in another office forwarded the call to Johnson. He picked up the phone and gave his name. After a short few seconds he hung up.

"Our presence is requested at operations," he said as he stood.

"O.K., we aren't wasting any time are we?" Stone said.

"No such thing in the SEAL's." Johnson said as they made their way to the side door and out to the parking lot where the detachment vehicles were parked. After a short drive, Stone and Johnson entered the front door of the operations building and presented themselves at the security desk. Stone's identification was verified and he was issued a temporary security badge. Once the security formalities were completed, Stone followed Johnson down a short hallway to a door with another security guard posted outside. After another review of Stone's credentials the door was buzzed open and the two men entered. The room was typical of operations facilities Stone had seen as a member of Special Forces and with the FBI Hostage Rescue Unit. On one wall was a large video screen surrounded by smaller screens each displayed either data or video depending on what was needed at the moment. At this time the large central screen bore a map of the Atlantic Ocean with symbols located in various places that were probably sea and aircraft.

On one of the smaller screens was an image of what appeared to be satellite images of a cargo vessel underway on a large body of water. On the floor, arranged in three concentric semi-circles were a series of computer terminals manned by personnel selected from all branches of the U.S. Military. The lights were dim to help the computer operators who sat for eight-hour shifts staring into monitors. The reduced light in the room helped protect their eyes from the strain of ambient light causing glare on the monitors. In the rear of the room, behind the semi-circles of computers was what appeared to be a watch officer at a desk. At this time a Navy commander occupied the seat, although the position could be manned by an officer of any branch of the service of similar rank. Behind the watch officers desk, along the rear wall were four conference rooms of which two were occupied. It was one of those rooms that a Navy lieutenant emerged and walked in the direction of Stone and Johnson.

"Hello Mr. Stone." O'Brien said. "My name is Max O'Brien SEAL

Platoon Commander."

"Pleasure to meet you," replied Stone. "Impressive facility you have here."

"Yea, these guys do a fantastic job. Our jobs would be a lot tougher it it wasn't for them. They amaze me. I couldn't stay cooped up in a dark room like this, I'd go nuts."

"Same here." Stone agreed.

"Well let's step into the conference room and we'll make sure we have our ducks in a row." Stone and the officers and several representatives from the Navy's Sixth Fleet spent the next few hours covering every aspect of the operation that was about to unfold. At the end of the meeting Stone, O'Brien and Johnson headed back to SEAL Headquarters and Stone retired to his room for a well deserved shower and a change of clothes. A good night's sleep and an early breakfast would be all Stone would be able to enjoy as a land lubber for the next few days.

* * * * * * *

The crew of the USS Anzio was just beginning a six month deployment to the Mediterranean and had just put to sea after a layover at Rota. She was only three hours to sea when she was ordered to return to Rota. When she docked she was to take on a SEAL platoon and several unidentified personnel. Her orders were vague. She would proceed southwest and intercept a civilian cargo ship where the SEAL team would carry out its orders. The Captain of the Anzio, Captain Raymond Oliver had just settled into his bunk for a few hours sleep when the order to return came in. Now with the receipt of the cryptic orders, he doubted that he'd be able to return to his near sleep condition until he learned what was actually going on. Oliver got up, dressed and headed for the wheelhouse. The weather was clear and his boat was running fine. He was proud of his command. His crew was competent and enthusiastic. As he walked he looked at every part of his boat. If he noticed anything that was not correct, he would mention it to his first officer and expected it to be taken care of. Next to his wife and children, the Anzio was the most important thing to him. Maybe it was that she would take care of him in an emergency if he takes care of her. Out on the sea there was nothing else but a man and his vessel, whether it was the deer skin canoe for the Native America or a 9600 ton guided missile cruiser. Man and machine depend on each other for survival when both are at the mercy of a forbidding sea.

Sitting in the Captains' chair in the wheel house of the Aegis guided missile cruiser, Oliver peered out over the structure that housed radar systems and other electronic intelligence assets of the modern warship. The sun would be coming up soon. The changes in orders felt like a huge waste of time to Oliver. But he knew there must be a good reason for the change. He leaned back in the chair and sipped on the cup of coffee that had been brought to him moments before. Oliver liked to be early for his appointments. He turned and asked the helmsman for a couple of more knots. The helmsman acknowledged with an "Aye" and slid the lever on the control panel a little further forward.

CHAPTER 15

Audrey felt a little better now. The ocean had calmed down. The sailing was smooth and the meals she ate were staying down and strengthening her body. She was able to think logically about her situation now. Even with her limited experience in the world she had come to the conclusion that she had been kidnapped. She had no idea where she was going and the length of the journey had no effect on her deliberations. To her, this type of trip was what happens to all people who are kidnapped. When she got where she was going she would meet all of the previous abductees and they would describe their individual cases and each story would be similar. All who had been kidnapped before her must have been on this boat also. Maybe they all got sick on the food as she did. She sat in the corner of her little cell with her arms wrapped around her legs as she considered all the possibilities of those that had gone before her. She wondered where they were now, knowing that she would be there soon also. She thought of her mother, father and sister. She fantasized that they would be there where ever she was going. Then a realization hit her, terrified her, no they would not be there. She would be alone and she would never see them again. She began to cry once more.

The crewman who had been bringing food to the people in the cells continued his work in the kitchen. He signed on with the Blue Star at its stop in the Bahamas. He had to get off the island. The last robbery he had committed was clean, he thought, but the police had been asking questions around his neighborhood and he was convinced they would soon get him. He couldn't figure out how they tracked him down, but they had. He had to leave. He didn't consider himself a thief or a dishonest person, but the condition he found himself in forced his decision to supplement his spartan income buy robbing small businesses. He was lucky to find the opening on the ship that he had seen in the port. He'd heard that they would hire locals to work on the ships on its passage across the Atlantic. He presented such a convincing image during his interview that he was hired. The ship needed a new kitchen hand because the last one had jumped ship in Galveston. Kitchen help was not exactly skilled labor so finding new hands was not difficult. Although keeping them was. Over the last eight hundred miles since being hired, Pedro learned his way around the galley. The work was hard. The hours were long. But he knew he could quit when he wanted.

His only regret was leaving Consuela. She was not a beautiful girl. But she worked hard at her brother's restaurant and she seemed to love Pedro. She would give him money when he had none, which was quite regularly. Instead of buying new clothes or a gift for Consuela, he would waste it all at the bar near a hotel that attracted guests from America and other wealthy countries. What he expected to find there he was unsure of. Maybe the idea of becoming more like the rich Americans attracted him. He especially liked to watch the young American girls as they went about their vacation rituals. They were beautiful creatures. Their hair was so beautiful. They were not fat like so many of the women he had come to know on his island. He approached a few over the years but they had ignored him. He began to feel unworthy. Why wouldn't they respect him? He had wondered.

Several times he was removed from the hotel property by the security guards. They threatened to arrest him if they saw him near the guests again. Pedro would wait a few weeks until he was sure the guards had been replaced or no longer remembered his face. Then he would return to the hotel. There was something about the light skin, the smell of perfumes, the young slender bodies that he couldn't resist.

The tourist girls were the cause of his career of robbing stores. He would wait until they closed for the day and break in. He got as much of the merchandise as he could run with and make his way to the docks. He would wait there until he was sure he was not followed and then he headed home. The following days he unloaded his haul where ever he could find a buyer. Much of his take ended up on tables at the bazaars that attracted the same tourists he was hoping to impress with his stolen fortune.

Pedro had noticed the young girl behind the metal door of her cell when he took her first meal. She looked as though she was the youngest of the group that were being transported in the cells. Each time he brought her food he tried to look through the little door as she took the plate from him. He hadn't said anything to her yet. She seemed so upset and then she was sick for several days. Being unaccustomed to the sea, Pedro had developed a little case of seasickness himself. But the pills the old man in the galley gave him relieved the symptoms. He needed to be at work. Illness was no excuse for not getting his assigned duties accomplished. He had been told that his work had to be finished or he would be put off at the next port and his pay would be forfeited. But, now he had his own little "tourist" girl to think and fantasize about. Every time he went to her cell to take food he thought about opening the door and going in. It wouldn't take long, he would be back at his post and no one would miss him. Maybe she would be nice to him. They were both lonely. She was locked up in that cold, dark cell and he was a prisoner on this ship just like she was, at least until he could get to another port. Maybe they would let them both off at the next stop. It was all just a fantasy. He knew that she was a prisoner for some reason. He had been told, very sternly, not to talk to any of the prisoners. Until now he had not talked to any of them. But as the hours went by he became more interested in the young American girl. He vowed that the next time he took her food that he would take a chance and talk to her, try to get to know her.

* * * * * * *

The Anzio made the return trip to Rota with appropriate haste. She was now docked at her mooring, receiving supplies and new equipment that belonged to the SEAL team that would be joining her shortly. The crew would get one nights rest before putting to sea for a second time in four days. This time the Anzio and her crew had a clearly defined mission. Instead of a simple patrol of the Mediterranean, she would actually be supporting a worthwhile mission. The members of the crew that had the need to know were visibly excited about being called on to support a SEAL mission. The word finally got around to the entire crew as to who would be coming aboard. This was the type of mission they all joined the Navy for. Captain Oliver understood what kind of effect this mission would have on his crew. He would like to have been able to brief the entire crew with the details, but in the interest of operations security, he was forced to wait until they put to sea to inform them of the ultimate mission of the Anzio and her crew. Captain Oliver was resting in his cabin when his phone rang.

"Sir, the loading of the supplies and gear is complete," the first officer said.

"Very well, I guess we can just sit tight until the SEAL team arrives."

"Aye, Aye," replied the first officer. Oliver heard the line click indicating that the other end had been hung up. He closed his eyes hoping to catch a few minutes of sleep before his attention was needed for some other matter. Oliver had not yet recovered from the lack of sleep during the preparations for the last sail and then to be recalled to the same port within two days was extremely stressful. He managed to drift off shortly after closing his eyes. His trust in his crews' ability to get their jobs done with proper attention to detail made it easy for him to rest.

While the Anzio was taking on its new supplies and gear, Lt. O'Brien's SEAL platoon was finalizing its operation plans. Russ Stone was involved in the planning of each phase of the operation. He would also accompany the boarding team onto the suspect vessel. Each team member was given a list of required gear and a description of his responsibilities during the boarding operation. The operation was practiced until it was regurgitated precisely by each team member. Soon Lt. O'Brien was satisfied with the performance of his team and he allowed them to return to their rooms for a few hours sleep. They each set their clocks for a four

AM awakening at which time they would board the Anzio for the first leg of the mission.

Before heading to his bunk, Stone found the nearest telephone. He dialed a series of numbers that would connect him to the Clarks home. He was unsure of the time in Atlanta, but he really didn't care and he was certain that the Clarks didn't either. After a few rings Tom Clark answered. Russ proceeded to explain to Tom as much as he could about what was about to take place halfway around the world. Russ explained with guarded optimism that within forty-eight hours Tom Clark may be able to speak to his daughter again. Russ was careful to point out that he was still not certain what he will actually find when they board and search the ship. But he thought the Clarks should know where the investigation was at this point in time.

"Thank you for the call, Russ." Tom Clark said. "Thank you for your hard work. If you find Audrey we would never be able to repay you for what you've done."

"Thank you, Tom." Russ said. "I sincerely hope that you will be talking to your daughter very soon."

After hanging up the phone, Russ hoped the call had not been premature. What if Audrey was not on board? What if there was evidence that she had been onboard but had not survived long enough to be rescued? How would he explain any of that to Tom and Rachel when he had been so positive? It was a chance that he had decided was worth taking. He was confident she was aboard the Blue Star, though he did not know her physical condition. Russ spared the Clarks the details of his concerns. He was as positive as he could be.

Four AM came quickly. The cool darkness enveloped the naval base like a damp blanket. The bus with its driver from the motor pool arrived at SEAL headquarters at three forty-five. By four twenty the SEAL team along with Russ Stone were loaded and on their way to the pier where the Anzio was moored. Like a huge grey ghost she loomed as she came slowly into view. By five AM all personnel were aboard and accounted for and a tugboat was pushing Oliver's vessel clear of her mooring and into the channel to begin her mission of mercy. Stone and O'Brien joined Captain Oliver on the bridge to watch the crewman perform their duties. The professionalism of the crew was impressive. The Anzio maneuvered as if she were a much smaller vessel. The helmsman coaxed her into the deeper channel and out into open sea as if he and the 9600-ton vessel were of one mind. Upon reaching the open sea a course was set that would bring them to a point that would intercept the Blue Star in approximately twelve hours. Convinced that everything was operating properly, Captain Oliver decided to retire to his cabin and continue to try to catch up on his sleep. Stone and O'Brien joined the rest of the SEAL team below to rehash the operation plan. Stones' military background and his experience with the FBI's Hostage Rescue Team along with his obvious military bearing convinced O'Brien that he would make a functional member of the team. Once O'Brien was certain the team was ready, he relieved them to return to their bunks to rest for the remainder of the voyage.

*　*　*　*　*　*　*

The cook finished preparing the morning meal for the crew of the Blue Star. They were nearly finished eating when he measured out the portions for the six "passengers" who were being held in the cells one deck below. Pedro was instructed to cease washing dishes and take the meals to the cells. Pedro dried his hands and picked up one of the trays and headed for the first cell. He had no idea how long this trip would take so he decided that today would be a good day to try to get to know the girl. He saved her meal for last so that he would have time to talk to her a little before the cook missed him.

After serving the first five, Pedro opened the little door on the last cell and slid the tray inside on the small platform. Instead of closing and locking the door, he left it open and watched as the girl took the tray, sat on her bunk and began to eat. She did not realize that the door had remained open and that someone was watching her. Pedro watched as she used her fingers to pick up the food and put it in her mouth. He thought she was very pretty. He watched in silence as she ate all of the food. Then she drank the water from the small cup and placed it back on the tray.

Audrey stood and moved toward the door to place the tray on the little shelf. She then went to the little sink and washed her face and hands. Pedro removed the tray from the shelf and set it gently on the floor beside him. He continued to watch her through the little slot in the door as she sat back down on the bed. Audrey had not yet noticed the little door was still open. The darkness of her cell and that of the hallway outside made it difficult for her to see anything with any clarity. Pedro continued to watch her as she picked her legs up and stretched out on the bed. He knew he did not have much time left so he decided to return to the galley so that he would be seen. He closed the little door and picked up the tray and climbed the stairs to the galley.

Audrey felt a little sleepy after the meal so she decided to take a nap. She was still unsure of the time and she did not know whether she had just eaten breakfast, lunch or dinner. She had no exercise so she was constantly tired. There was really nothing else to do but sleep, eat and think. Since thinking tended to make her sad, she decided to sleep. She had just closed her eyes when she heard the little door on the cell door click shut. She opened her eyes and looked in that direction. She had not paid any attention to the door before. Now she couldn't remember if it had been shut while she was eating. She did remember the tray being removed as it always was by an unknown person who never says anything. Audrey looked into the semi darkness at the little door. She could barely see it. She suddenly came to the realization that someone could have been looking at her through the little door while she was eating. Audrey shivered with fright and pulled the thin sheet over her entire body and stared at the little hole in the door.

* * * * * * *

The weather was clear and bright. The ocean was smooth and the Anzio was operating perfectly. The big ship was making around fourteen knots southwest on an intercept course with her prey. Russ Stone was enjoying the trip. He stood on the deck on the starboard side and watched the sea go by. Soon Lt. O'Brien arrived from below and found a position next to Stone at the rail. He stood silent for a moment.

"Man, I love the ocean." O'Brien said. Russ Stone was enjoying the view and the ride, but he was not quite as excited as O'Brien obviously was.

"Yea, this is nice. I just don't get to see as much of it as you do." Stone said. "I usually experience the ocean from the shore or from thirty-five thousand feet. Being this close with no land in sight takes a little getting used to."

"I can understand that." O'Brien said. "I spend a lot of time out here. Not as much as the captain and the crew of this boat, but I have grown to love the sea." Stone listened as O'Brien seemed to be enjoying himself and Stone had not seen him this relaxed since he met him. "I don't believe I could live away from the ocean. When I leave the Navy I will have to stay close to it." Stone remembered the times he went out on the Chesapeake Bay with Bill Barnes. They would take the wives and spend all day on Bill's sailboat. Helping Bill the little he could was an excellent experience. But he was always within sight of the shore. Maybe that was part of the reason he had joined the Army instead of the Navy. He was used to tromping through the woods near his home scaring up quail or sitting in a stand waiting for a buck to cross his line of sight. He grew up on the ground, in the woods. Later during high school he learned the art of backpacking. He and friends would do weekend trips along the Appalachian Trail and many of the lesser known trails that intersect it. He enjoyed the animals he would see along the trail. The occasional bear, the snake that slithered across your path, the raccoon that climbed down the chimney of your backwoods shelter and disrupted all of your pots and pans looking for food at three o'clock in the morning.

One night while camping at the base of a three thousand foot mountain in western North Carolina, he heard a noise like nothing he ever heard before. Russ tried to match it to obvious animals that may inhabit the area: black bear, puma, a wild dog or a wild pig. Nothing seemed to fit. The identity of the animal that made the noise evaded him. He continued to walk up the mountain the next day without thinking of that noise again. It wasn't until many years later that he heard that noise again and it was from an unexpected source. While watching television one night he ran across a special on Bigfoot, Sasquatch, Yeti, and some of the vocalizations that were aired on the program took him back to that night at the base of that mountain. The more he thought about the noise he heard that night the more he realized that it was similar to the vocalizations they were airing on that television special. Since seeing that program he had wondered if it was a Sasquatch on that mountain that night above his camp. The possibility of a North American Ape has intrigued him since.

"I grew up in the woods and joined the Army after high school." Stone said. "I'm a land lubber, I admit that fully." O'Brien smiled.

* * * * * * *

Pedro knew he had to clean up the kitchen but he believed that he had time to return to the little girls' cell before anyone started looking for him. If he raised the curiosity of the cook he could just tell him that he had become sick and had to remain in the head a while. His mind developed a series of excuses as to why he was gone so long and had not cleaned the galley as he was supposed to. He was beginning to feel a certain nervous excitement since deciding to visit the girl. He fantasized about her liking him quickly and them both helping each other cure their loneliness. Pedro was sure that once she got to know him that she would find him friendly and a good lover. All of the other girls he had known told him so. Why should she be any different? Besides, she had to be so lonely, being locked up in that cell for so many days now. He was sure that she would be glad to have some company for a little while. Pedro was enjoying his fantasies. He made his way toward the stairs leading down to the cells. He was sure no one had seen him leave. He had plenty of time he thought. As long as the girl was smart enough to take advantage of the time they had, everything would be fine.

Pedro approached the door of the cell. He was more concerned with one of the crew seeing him there than he was of the girl hearing him. He had been told not to talk to any of the people in the cells or he would be thrown over the side of the ship. He really didn't believe the threat from the crewman who told him that. He really didn't believe they would throw him into the ocean. They would probably just fire him and put him off in a strange country. Pedro didn't care. He looked at the lock on the door. In the dim light it was difficult to see. He noticed that there was no lock. It was fastened closed with just a large bolt. Upon closer inspection he saw a small latch that held the bolt closed. It was more to keep the bolt from working its way out from the vibrations of the machinery than to provide security. As quietly as he could he lifted the small latch and slowly slid the bolt out of its hole.

* * * * * * *

Inside the cell Audrey had calmed down a little and was lying on the bunk with her eyes wide open. She could not sleep now. She was thinking of her family when she suddenly heard something on the door click. She focused all of her senses on the door. Unconsciously she eliminated all sensory input except her vision and hearing, which seemed to rise to extreme levels. Her field of vision narrowed to include only the cell door. She became terrified, unable to speak much less scream. She stared wide-eyed as the door seemed to narrow. A dark margin began to grow on the left side of the door. The door was opening she finally understood. Audrey tried to scream. That door had not been opened since she woke up in the cell so many days before. The dark margin widened but she could not see anything beyond the plane of the doorframe. She stared into the darkness unable to make any kind of noise. All she could do was stare into the void where the door had been. Suddenly, an orb began to come into focus in the darkness. She could only scream inside, as the orb started to take on the appearance of a human face. With tears flowing, she eventually realized that a person was standing in the darkness of her cell door.

CHAPTER 16

The Blue Star had finally revealed itself as a blip on the Anzio's radar screen. She had emerged from the clouds and fog exactly where she was projected to be. Stone and the SEAL team were below getting into their tactical uniforms and checking out the equipment when the word came from the First Mate that the Blue Star had been spotted. The team gathered its equipment and they made their way topside and loaded everything into the SH-60 Seahawk helicopter that was waiting to take them over to the deck of the Blue Star. The Seahawk was the Navy's version of the Army's UH-60 Blackhawk helicopter. The versatility of this aircraft made it a welcomed addition to all of the branches of the U.S. Armed Forces. The navy used the twin-engine Seahawk for anti-submarine warfare, search and rescue, drug interdiction as well as special ops.

It would be another thirty minutes before the Anzio was in the immediate vicinity of the Blue Star. It was planned not to communicate with the Blue Star and just let her think the two ships were just crossing paths. The insertion of the SEAL team would be the first thing the captain of the Blue Star would see that would indicate his ship was the subject of a boarding. Inside the Seahawk, Lt. O'Brien's team was secure and ready for flight operations. The pilot of the bird radioed his readiness for takeoff to Captain Oliver who gave him the go ahead.

The Seahawk lifted off from its pad on the bow of the Anzio and tilted in the direction of the Blue Star. She would fly just above the surface of the ocean until it reached the freighter. Hopefully the navigator would not be too attentive and alert the captain of the Blue Star until the

SEAL team was on her deck.

* * * * * * *

Audrey stared at the apparition as she sobbed hoping that it would disappear. She could not move to pull the sheet over her head. Her sobbing was becoming louder although she could not discern the volume herself. She began to make out features in the face as if it were getting closer. In fact it was getting closer. Pedro was moving slowly into the cell. At the same time he began talking to Audrey in his broken English.

"Be quiet, I am friend. Be quiet, I am Friend," he said. Audrey began to see the mouth moving but she could not hear any words. Her fear had overridden her sense of hearing. Pedro moved completely into the room and pulled the door closed behind him. He glanced around the room to become more familiar with his surroundings. He had not been in any of the cells where the prisoners were being held. He had only seen them from the outside when he delivered their food. His vision returned to the girl lying on the bunk. He could see her better now that he was in the room. She was covered in the sheet and she was obviously terrified. He stepped closer to the bunk and knelt down beside it.

Be quiet, I am friend." Pedro said again, as he moved his hand to her shoulder. He could feel the girl trembling. Pedro knew he did not have much time. He gripped the sheet and tried to pull it free of her grip. Audrey's sobbing became a little louder but Pedro was not worried as the whining of the engines drowned any noises she could make short of screaming and that could only be heard in the hallway outside of the door. "Please, be quiet, I am friend to you." Pedro said into the girls' wide eyes as he tugged on the sheet a little harder.

* * * * * * *

The Seahawk with its compliment of Special Ops personnel was approaching the Blue Star at top speed. The aircraft was just barely above the surface of the water. Hopefully the tactics employed by the helicopter pilot would be stealthy enough to prevent anyone onboard the freighter from notifying anyone onshore of the boarding. The pilot of the Sea-hawk was an expert in the insertion of Special Ops teams. When the chopper was barely fifty yards from the port side of the vessel, he flared up and dropped down onto one of the hatch covers of the Blue Star. Within fifteen seconds the SEAL team with their AR15-A2's at the tactical position, had disembarked and were making their way to each members' assigned position. O'Brien, Stone and two team members headed for the wheelhouse. Three team members made their way to the door that accessed the lower levels of the ship. They were to begin the search of the vessel. The third team secured the deck of the Blue Star and then would join the second team and help with the search. Thirty seconds after touchdown on the freighters deck, O'Brien and Stone entered the wheelhouse. With their weapons at the ready with sights aligned they caught the lazy crewmen at the helm of the Blue Star off guard. The next thing the crewmen knew they were being told to lie on the floor and put their hands behind their heads. O'Brien stepped over to the helm and killed the engines. There were only two crewmen in the wheelhouse and Stone did not believe either one of them was the captain. He kicked the one that had been sitting in the captain's chair.

"Where is your captain?" he said with the muzzle of his weapon pointed at the side of his head. The crewman saw no reason to resist the obvious superior force.

"In his cabin," he answered hoping that it was the correct answer considering his English was not very good and he was not exactly sure what the question was but he did recognize "captain." Stone turned to-ward O'Brien.

"I'm going below." Stone said.

"O.K., I believe we can handle things here." O'Brien replied sarcasti-cally, recognizing there was little threat from the two characters they had just thrown on the floor. Stone turned towards the door and slid down the stairs and disappeared through the door into the belly of the Blue Star. Stone could barely see as he entered the doorway below the wheel-house. He immediately came upon the radio room where one of the

SEALs was stationed. Stone got a thumbs up, indicating the room was secure. He had heard over his personal communications device shortly after claiming the wheelhouse that no one was found in the radio room so there was a good chance that no messages were sent concerning the boarding.

Stone continued aft hoping to find the captain's cabin. He heard a crackling from his earpiece and then a statement from the leader of the search squad announcing that the captain was secured in his cabin. Stone made his way to the cabin. When he arrived he found the captain in his underwear with his hands tied behind his back and a SEAL standing guard. Stone moved forward and stared into the face of the captain.

"Where are the prisoners?" Stone asked in a determined voice.

"You have no right to board my ship. We are in international waters and have violated no laws," mumbled the captain. Stone leveled his rifle at the captain's left eye.

"I've asked you a question and I expect an answer." He said as he flipped the selector switch on the rifle over to semi-automatic. The clicking of the rifles' selector switch must have done the trick. The captain of the Blue Star took a deep breath and resigned himself to the fact that there would be no negotiation with these people.

"They are below the galley," he finally said. Stone immediately left the cabin to make his way two decks down to the cells.

* * * * * * *

Pedro heard a thud from above. He had not heard a noise like that since he had been on the ship. But he had not heard anyone calling him so he continued to believe that he had time. He began to talk to the girl in his broken English.

"I am friend, I want to help you." He finally was able to get Audrey to release the grip on the sheet and he pulled it down to her waist. He put his hand on her shoulder.

"It's O.K., I am friend." He said looking deep into her frightened eyes.

Audrey had stared at the man from the time he entered the room. She was scared but she wanted to believe that he could really be her friend. Maybe he was there to help her escape and get back to her family. She relaxed a little and let him remove the sheet that she had tugged so tightly around her shoulders. She continued to sob uncontrollably, but she decided to trust him a little.

"My name is Audrey," she said softly.

Pedro's eyes widened with pleasure as he realized that he was getting somewhere. Pedro slowly moved his head closer to hers so that his lips were only a few inches from her face. He slowly reached out and put his right hand on her waist. Audrey flinched. Pedro heard a creaking noise behind him. Pedro turned his head just in time to see the butt of an AR-15 moving quickly toward his head, the impact sent him sprawling unconscious into the corner of the cell.

* * * * * * *

O'Brien stood in the wheelhouse and listened as each SEAL squad reported their status. Eventually all of the ship had been searched and all of her crew was in custody. O'Brien reported his platoon's status to the captain of the Anzio who then relaxed the alert status of his vessel. Stone and two of the SEALs found all of the prisoners and released them. The kidnapped girls were given a cursory check to make sure they could make the short helicopter ride over to the Anzio where the ship's medical officer would conduct a more thorough exam. They were obviously mistreated and malnourished. But they showed very little physical harm, which was surprising to the rescuers. As with Audrey, the other five prisoners were all female and seemed in age from twelve to sixteen years. The SEALs escorted all but Audrey to the helicopter that was still perched on top of the hatch cover in the middle of the Blue Star.

Stone bound the hands of the unconscious crewman lying in the corner and then found another blanket and wrapped it around Audrey. He knelt down beside her bunk and helped her to sit up. Audrey was still crying softly. He pulled a bandana out of his pocket and wiped away a few tears.

"Audrey, my name is Russell Stone," he said. "Are you all right?" Audrey looked at the man kneeling beside the bed. She was not sure what to believe. She thought that the other man was her friend too. Stone looked her over and did not see any obvious injuries. "Audrey, your mom and dad have sent me to find you. They have missed you very much." She looked into Stone's eyes and tried to smile.

"My mom and dad?" she asked tentatively.

"Yes, they are waiting for you." Stone said reassuringly. "They love you very much and they want you to come home." Audrey smiled a little. Then she looked over at the unconscious man in the corner. Audrey was quickly realizing that her ordeal may be over and that she may soon be reunited with her family. She laid her head on Stones' shoulder and he gave her a reassuring hug. So very few of his missions end as positively as this one had. He was content for the moment to cherish the success and the relief both of them felt.

"Where are my mom and dad?" Audrey finally asked.

"They are at home right now. We will call them in a little while and let you talk to them, O.K." Stone said.

"O.K." Audrey replied. "I'm hungry. Can we get something to eat before you take me home?" Russ Stone wanted to laugh. He was happy! He moved himself away from her and held her by the shoulders.

"Yes, we will get you as much as you can eat," he said with a smile and a little chuckle. Stone admired the fortitude of the little girl. Considering the ordeal she had been through, her spirit was good.

"I like pancakes." Audrey said trying to smile.

"I know a guy who loves to make pancakes and I'll bet he will make stacks of them for you, he'll make them until you can't eat anymore." Russ said thinking of the cook aboard the Anzio.

"Good, 'cause I'm hungry. I hated the food they gave me here." Audrey said. Stone looked around the little room she had been kept in. It was not clean and it was cold and damp.

"Let's go upstairs. I think that there is a ride waiting for you that will take you where the pancakes are." Russ helped Audrey to her feet and guided her out the door and up the stairs into the sunshine.

It was becoming a beautiful day. Audrey squinted her eyes tightly and shielded them with her hand as she emerged from the steel dungeon that had held her for so many terrible days. She looked around the deck at the other people there. She saw a few others who looked like they may have been held on the ship like she was. There were more people in dark suits and carrying guns like Mr. Stone and they were helping the other girls get into a helicopter. The helicopter was sitting on the middle of the ship like a huge grey bird.

"Let's get you on the helicopter." Stone said as he held Audrey close to him.

"O.K.," She said. He walked with her and helped her up over the edge of the cargo cover and then up into the helicopter. Audrey seemed a little cautious about riding on the helicopter. She had ridden on airplanes but not in a helicopter.

"Audrey, I'm going to stay here on this ship for a while." Stone said. "These men will take good care of you. You do what they say, O.K.?"

"Where are we going?" Audrey asked.

"You're going over to that ship." Stone pointed to the big, grey ship a few hundred yards away. "That is an American Navy ship and there is a doctor over there and he is going to check you over. Then they will get you some clean clothes and some pancakes. O.K." As Stone mentioned the pancakes he looked at one of the SEAL's as if to make sure he let the cook know that somebody needed to get some pancakes on the grill for this little girl.

"O.K., but when will I get to see my mom?" Audrey asked.

"We will call her very soon, O.K." Stone said. But first you need to get over to the other ship, it is safer over there. O.K.?" Stone said looking into Audrey's' eyes.

"O.K." Audrey answered obviously concerned about flying on the helicopter.

"Now, this helicopter is going to make a lot of noise, but you don't worry about it. Everything is going to be fine." He patted her on the shoulder hoping she would not be afraid on the short flight to the An- zio. Stone nodded to the pilot letting him know that everyone was on board and he could make his delivery. Stone stepped away from the chopper and the crew chief slid the door closed.

Russ Stone looked at the little girl through the window and smiled. He raised his hand and waved to her. She waved back as the pilot started the engines, brought the rotors up to the proper speed and lifted off the deck and made its way gracefully toward the waiting Navy vessel.

* * * * * * *

Stone turned and walked up to the wheelhouse. There he found O'Brien having a heart to heart discussion with the captain of the Blue Star, who had managed to find his clothing before being taken from his cabin to the wheelhouse. The rest of the crew had been collected in the galley and were under guard by two squads of the SEAL platoon. Stone stood back and listened while O'Brien explained the facts of life to the captain and his first mate.

O'Brien seemed to be making progress with the two crewmen. They seemed authentically afraid of the situation they were in. O'Brien made it clear to them that if they cooperated there was a good chance they would probably survive. Stone turned toward the window and watched as the Seahawk helicopter made its approach and landed gracefully on the Anzio. O'Brien seemed to be making headway with the two men who were, until a short time ago, in command of their vessel. Now it was clear that their captors were in command and it was in their best interest to listen closely to their newly assigned orders. The captain and his first mate were finally convinced that if they cooperated they would not be returned to the United States and prosecuted for transporting American citizens against their will.

The Blue Star would eventually be allowed to continue its voyage and it would deliver its cargo at the ports where she was scheduled to dock. The captain would resume command of the ship and essential members of the crew would be allowed to assume their respective positions. The captain and the crew would be able to receive the pay earned for the voyage, as long as they did as they were told. Stone turned again toward the Anzio and watched as the Seahawk lifted off again from the deck and tilted in the direction of the Blue Star.

"I'll go help get things organized on deck." Stone said to O'Brien.

"Have someone bring my gear up here, please."

"Sure." Stone said. He made his way down to the deck where four SEALs where unloading gear from the helicopter. Seated in the Seahawk now were six females who were dressed in street clothes, but they had a gleam in their eyes that was illustrative of their professionalism and determination to see their mission through to a successful conclusion. The gear was off loaded and the six undercover "kidnapped" hostages disembarked. The six women were volunteers from several agencies of the federal government. Two were from the FBI's Hostage Rescue Team, three were Air Force elite Delta Force and the last girl was a CIA operative. It was obvious to Stone that these girls were in top physical condition and they all looked younger than their actual ages.

These girls can take care of themselves. Stone thought. They were all well trained and confident in their abilities. They had flown out to meet the Anzio after she was already underway. He greeted each one as they exited the helicopter, and then a SEAL member escorted them to the bunk area that had been found for them below on the same deck as the galley. Stone smiled as the women picked up their own gear, not allowing the SEAL members to complete a gentlemanly gesture of carrying the gear for them. He was happy that the agencies involved had agreed to follow through and attempt to locate the people responsible for the kidnapping and transport of the six kids that had been rescued earlier.

CHAPTER 17

A team of psychologists and counselors met the helicopter as it touched down on the Anzio with the six rescued kids. They were each debriefed and given a complete medical examination. Audrey and Janet, her counselor, were now in the galley munching on a stack of pancakes. The other five abductees thought the idea of pancakes sounded good so they were enjoying their own.

"These pancakes are good. That was a good idea you had." Janet said.

"Yeah, pancakes are my favorite." Audrey replied through a mouthful.

"How are you feeling, Audrey?" Janet asked with a tone of concern in her voice. Audrey was a strong little girl. She had been a little more quiet than Janet expected. She appreciated Janet being there to talk to her.

"I feel good," she said, "why did those men take me and put me on those boats?" This was why the girls were provided counselors. To answer questions like these and to help them come to terms with the ordeal they had gone through.

"I don't know why they did that, Audrey. But you are safe now. You don't have to worry about those men anymore. We are going to take care of you and get you back to your mom and dad as soon as we can." Audrey looked into Janet's smiling eyes.

"Thanks." Audrey said. "When can we call my mom and dad?"

"As soon as we get done eating we can go to the communications center and call them." Janet reassured her.

"Great, I can't wait." Audrey said with enthusiasm. Then she picked up the pace of her eating.

* * * * * * *

On board the Blue Star Stone had utilized its satellite phone and made a call to Atlanta. Rachel answered the phone.

"Rachel, this is Russ Stone." He said.

"Hello, Russ." Rachel was afraid to ask anything else.

"Rachel, we have found Audrey." Russ said then quickly said. "She's fine." He didn't want Rachel to assume the worse.

"Oh, my God!" Stone heard through the receiver. "Is she alright?" Then he heard her yell for Tom to pick up another phone.

"Hello Russ, this is Tom. Did you find her?" Russ didn't have time to answer as Rachel answered for him.

"Yes, they found her!" Rachel said with a shaky voice.

"Thank God." Tom said. "Where is she? Can we talk to her?" Russ was having difficulty trying to say anything.

"O.K., calm down for a minute and let me fill you in," he said.

"O.K." Tom and Rachel said simultaneously.

"I can't go into specifics, but right now Audrey is on a Navy ship in the Atlantic." Russ continued. "She is being looked over by medical personnel…." Russ was not finished when Rachel cut in.

"No, is something wrong with her?" She said becoming afraid.

"No, no, I looked her over myself and she looks fine. I don't think there is anything to be concerned about." Russ said trying to calm Rachel. "Once they check her out, they will give her some food. Pancakes, she asked for pancakes."

"That's her favorite." Tom said sounding happy. Russ could hear Rachel breathing heavily, probably trying to control her emotions.

"Now, the plan is," continued Russ, "to get her back to Rota, Spain, the naval base there. You guys get your tickets so you can meet her there." Russ said.

146

"We will leave now." Tom said.

"That's good Tom," Russ said. "Also I believe they will be calling so you can talk to Audrey soon. So let's hang up so they can get through. O.K."

"O.K." Tom said.

"Thank you so much." Rachel said.

"Goodbye for now." Russ said and hung up the phone. Russ felt good. It was a damn good day. He leaned back against the desk in the radio room and enjoyed the feeling. He reveled in the extreme sense of pride he'd earned by being able to reunite a family after such a terrible experience. His PCU crackled in his ear interrupting his moment of peace.

"All team members, we will be getting underway within the hour." The voice of Lt. O'Brien said over the communications system. "Secure all gear and review your checklists. Out."

The unnecessary crewmen of the Blue Star had been locked in the cells that originally contained the abductees. The captain, the cook and the engineer were allowed to perform their duties. The SEALs had changed out of their tactical gear and were now wearing the clothing similar to any seaman who would crew a vessel like the Blue Star. O'Brien assumed the position of first mate and along with the captain prepared the vessel to continue its voyage.

Two SEALs took control of the engine room and never let the engineer out of their sight. The cook was allowed to continue with his responsibilities although he now had twice as many mouths to feed. The rations had to be cut so the food would last.

One SEAL worked in the galley and was the envy of the rest of the platoon. Stone and the remaining SEAL's were to monitor the radio and the other functions of the ship.

On board the Anzio, Audrey, along with her new friend Janet left the galley and made their way to the communications room. They were escorted to a desk with a computer terminal and several phones. As Audrey approached she noticed a lady sitting at the desk smiling at her.

"Do you want to call your mom and dad, Audrey?" She asked.

"Yes, please." Audrey answered.

"O.K.," said the lady. "What is your phone number?" Audrey gave her the number to her house and the lady picked up one of the phones and punched on the computer keyboard. Audrey watched with interest because she had never seen a phone like this. After a few seconds the lady looked at Audrey and said.

"Is this the Clark residence?" Audrey could not hear the reply. "Good," said the lady. "This is Petty Officer Teresa Stanton aboard the USS Anzio. I have your daughter here and she would like to speak to you." Stanton handed the phone to Audrey.

'Hello." Audrey said. Tom and Rachel were in the living room along with Rachel's mother and Melissa. Rachel was barely able to control her emotions as she heard Audrey on the phone. Tom had his arm around her and held her tightly.

"Hello baby." Rachel finally said. "Are you alright?" Audrey smiled upon hearing he mother's voice.

"Yea, I'm alright. When can I come home?" Audrey asked.

"Soon, very soon." Rachel said on the verge of tears. "Daddy and I are catching a plane and we will be there soon to bring you home, O.K. baby." Rachel looked up at Tom and gave him a nervous smile. "Do you want to speak to daddy?"

"Yea." Audrey said. She looked at Janet and Teresa and smiled.

"Hello sweetheart." Audrey heard through the phone.

"Hello daddy." Audrey said. "I'm sorry for all of this trouble." She knew how much her father wanted everything to be done right and he doesn't like problems. Tom felt an ache in his heart when he heard her say that.

"That's O.K. honey. It's not your fault I love you so much. We can't wait to see you."

"I love you too," said Audrey.

"Do you want to speak to Melissa and Granny?" Tom asked.

"Yea. Sure." Tom handed the phone to Melissa and the girls talked for a few minutes and then it was granny's turn. Audrey had a big smile on her face as she told the story about flying on the helicopter and riding on the big Navy ship. She said that she had never seen the ocean when there was no shore around. After everyone had spoken to Audrey, Rachel took the phone.

"Honey, we will be there soon to get you, O.K. Now you be careful until we get there." Rachel concluded with tears in her eyes. Then everybody told Audrey goodbye as Rachel held the phone out so Audrey could here everyone. Rachel put the phone back to her ear and said, "I love you, Audrey."

"I love you too, Mom, bye." Audrey said.

"Bye, sweetheart." Rachel said finally and she slowly hung up the phone. As she did she began to cry. Tom held her and Melissa tightly.

* * * * * * *

Audrey handed the phone back to Teresa. "Thank you," she said as Teresa took the phone.

"Audrey." Janet said. "We have a few more things to do before we can leave the ship, O.K." She knew there was a little more therapy Audrey would need. She was hoping that talking about her ordeal would help her come to terms with it. It would be about ten hours before the Clarks would arrive at Rota to pick up Audrey and the helicopter ride from the Anzio to Rota would only take about three hours. Janet would accompany her on the helicopter ride and stay by her side until she could turn her over to her parents. So Janet and Audrey went back to Janet's cabin to talk.

* * * * * * *

The Blue Star was underway and resumed its original course. The Anzio would tail her by a few miles as the two ships made their way to the Blue Star's first stop in the Mediterranean, Port Said, where the "new" hostages would be turned over to their next abductors. The Anzio would take up station a few miles off shore where it would become the command post for the operation to capture as many members of the kidnapping ring as they could. The men of the SEAL platoon and Russ Stone had a few days of sailing in front of them before they reached Port Said. They were able to use that time to rehearse the mission and get their gear and equipment in operating order. Russ Stone knew that Audrey was in good hands. He was sorry that he was not going to be able to be there when she and her family were reunited. He had called again and explained everything to the Clarks and they were all for tracking down and capturing the men that did this to their daughter. Russ promised that he would come see them the next time he was in Atlanta.

Russ stood in the wheelhouse and watched as the big ship plowed the seas. It was another beautiful day and Russ felt good. He looked over at O'Brien who was going over a few details with the captain of the Blue Star. He realized how lucky Audrey and her family were. To be able to have men like O'Brien, Captain Oliver and the rest of the SEAL platoon on their side was too good to be true. He wished he could call on this kind of support on every missing person's case that he worked. If it had not been for finding the My Marie and realizing that there was more than one victim involved he would have been all alone and Audrey would not have had the same chance of being found. Russ began to think about his own family. He walked over to O'Brien and slapped him on the back. Oliver turned and Russ shook his hand.

"Thanks for what you are doing." Russ said. "It's a good thing we have done here today." O'Brien looked at Russ and squeezed his hand.

"This is the most gratifying mission I have ever been on." O'Brien said. "I look forward to catching as many of these bastards as we can."

"That will be a good day too." Russ said. "I'll let you get back to work. I'm going below to make a phone call." Russ headed for the radio room where he planned to make a phone call of his own.

* * * * * * *

The atmosphere around the Clark house was a mixture of excitement and confusion. Tom and Rachel were hurriedly packing for their trip. Tom called the airlines as soon as they hung up after talking to the Navy personnel at Rota, Spain. The Naval personnel were preparing to receive the kidnapped girls from the Anzio and their families who were flying in from the states. Several of the girls were going to meet their families on the east coast of the U.S. Tom and Rachel decided to go get their daughter. Melissa and her grandmother were trying to help them pack but they only seemed to be getting in the way. So they decided to just stand back and watch. Eventually, the packing was finished and Melissa got kisses from her parents.

"You be good and listen to your grandmother." Rachel said to her daughter.

"I will." Melissa said. "Bye, Bye." Rachel got into the car. Tom started the engine and backed out of the driveway as the four of them waved to each other. It was very early in the morning and as soon as Tom and Rachel settled into the drive to the airport, the time began to reveal itself. She and Tom were excited about going to bring their daughter home, but they were also looking forward to getting on the plane so they could finish the night's sleep that had been interrupted by the phone call from the Anzio.

* * * * * * *

Russell Stone and Lt. O'Brien sat across from each other at a table in the galley of the Blue Star. Satellite photos and other documents were spread on the table between them. The deception will have to be executed flawlessly. Otherwise the lives of the undercover operatives will be at stake. The two men had sat in the same spot for the past four hours going over each detail of the operation. Neither man was the type to leave anything to chance. They would rack their brains to expose any problem in the plan. So far though they had been unable to find any errors in the op-plan created by Central Command (CENTCOM) headquarters. The plan, created by computer and reviewed by strategists at CENTCOM at McDill Air Force Base in Florida, was faxed to the radio room aboard the Blue Star.

"It's time for more coffee." Stone said.

"I concur." O'Brien replied as Stone rose from his stool, grabbed both men's coffee cups and filled them at the counter.

"I just hope that the off loading of the prisoners is done at Port Said." Stone remarked as he stepped back to the table with the coffee. "The more our people are exposed to the locals in the port, the more risky things get."

"You're right, we'll just have to get in as much practice acting like real crew of this tub before we get there," answered O'Brien. "We have two more days of practice and the crew is surprisingly helpful." Russ laughed and acknowledged.

"Yea, I believe we put a sufficient amount of fear in them. These guys are just commercial sailors. They are only here for a paycheck, not to fight somebody else's battle." Russ took a sip of coffee and picked up one of the satellite photos. "How certain are you that our credentials will be right?" The credentials were being prepared at CIA headquarters at Langley and would be flown by an Air Force F-15 to Rota, Spain, then helicoptered out to the Blue Star. The credentials would be used by the SEALs to cross international borders once they were on the ground in the Middle East.

"My experience is that the guys at Langley are the best in the world at crafting a fake I.D." O'Brien answered. "We shouldn't have any problems crossing borders as long as we play our parts correctly." O'Brien had several excursions similar to this one under his belt. He had a couple of months experience operating among the populace on the streets of Beirut, Jerusalem and Bagdad.

"Glad to hear that," sighed Stone. 'This will be my first time playing a local in Egypt. I hope I don't disappoint you."

"Just do what I've told you," assured O'Brien. "and you won't have any problems. Just keep your head down and don't make eye contact with anyone."

* * * * * * *

The SEAL platoon along with Stone would pretend to be migrant workers traveling in an old truck to a new work site. Not knowing what direction the prisoners would be taken, they would be forced to play the tailing of them by ear. Three of the SEALs were Arab linguists. The others would act as itinerant workers. The undercover prisoners would be electronically tagged so they could be tracked by satellite and monitored by O'Brien on the ground. The command post aboard the Anzio would monitor the entire operation twenty-four seven. There would be two Seahawks standing by prepared to extract the SEALs on a moments notice. The other ships that had been tasked to provide support were making their way to the Port Said area. They would contain equipment and services that the Anzio did not, including specialized medical and airlift capabilities. The positioning of U.S. warships at any location in the Mediterranean was not unusual. So the arrival of them should not cause any alarm.

"I can't think of anything we have missed." O'Brien said.

"Me neither." Stone agreed.

"I will schedule several more training sessions with the platoon over the next forty-eight hours. Let's get some rest now. O.K? I could use some shuteye."

"Fine with me." Stone said, realizing that he had not had much sleep since his arrival at Rota. The men left the galley and made their way to their respective cabins for a little much needed rest. As he left the galley, O'Brien contacted his squad leaders and informed them of the times for the training sessions where they would rehearse the mission until it was known by heart.

* * * * * * *

Ben Fletcher sat comfortably as he listened to the Washington Symphony Orchestra perform Vivaldi's Four Seasons. He suddenly felt his beeper begin to vibrate. He stood, straightened his tuxedo jacket and leaned over to tell his wife that he would be right back. Once in the lobby he dialed the number from the beeper. He recognized the number as belonging to Bill Barnes. It rang once and was answered.

"Bill, how's it going?" Fletcher inquired.

"Hello Ben." Barnes replied. "Excellent. The hostages have been re-covered, all in good shape. They are being debriefed and arrangements are being made to get them home to their families."

"That's great Bill. And the follow-up mission?"

"On schedule and going smoothly so far." Barnes replied. "The tricky part is yet to come but I have all the confidence in O'Brien and Stone. It should go off without a hitch."

"Excellent, keep me informed, O.K. Bill." Fletcher said.

'Yes sir." Barnes replied and they hung up the phones. Ben Fletcher made his way back down the aisle and rejoined his wife. After the con-cert he would notify the director of the status of the operation. Now, though he would enjoy the rest of the concert.

* * * * * * *

The 747 touched down at Charles Degaulle International Airport and taxied up to the terminal. Tom and Rachel exited the aircraft and made their way as quickly as possible toward the gate where they had been told they would board a military plane bound for Rota. While the Clarks were over the Atlantic, Audrey had been helicoptered from the Anzio to Rota. The flight from the U.S. to Paris had been stressful for the Clarks. They were, of course, happy that their daughter was free and in good hands, but they wanted her with them. Rachel Clark wanted to hold her child. She cried much of the way across the Atlantic and Tom felt as though he needed to comfort her. The sleep they had hoped to get had not come. They both had many questions and terrible thoughts running though their minds. Was she really O.K.? Did they hurt her physically? Was she sexually assaulted? They were afraid the Navy had not told them everything. Maybe they were waiting until they had them there in person before they would get the whole story.

The airport was crowded. Tom and Rachel found an airline employee who gave them directions to the gate they were looking for. They knew the airplane waiting for them would not leave without them but they hurried anyway. A few minutes later they arrived at the gate and were met by a smiling face of a Navy sailor. She introduced herself and lead them through a door and out onto the tarmac where a small grey jet sat. The stairs were lowered and the sailor escorted them aboard and seated them.

"The pilots will be here in a moment and we will be off and in Rota in about an hour and a half," the sailor said. "Is there anything I can get you? We have sodas and a few snacks in the galley."

"Yea, I could use a Coke and some peanuts or crackers if you have any." Tom said.

"Same for me, please." Rachel said.

"I'll be right back," the sailor said with a smile and went to the rear of the plane. A few seconds later two men came through the door of the plane and introduced themselves as the pilots. One turned and raised the stairwell and closed the door. They briefly described the flight path they would be taking and the altitude they would be flying and then went forward into the cockpit. The sailor arrived with the drinks and snacks.

"If there is anything else you need just let me know," she said. Soon the engines started and they began to taxi toward the runway. Tom watched as the jet lined up with the runway and began its roll. Soon the jet lifted off the runway and gained altitude. After several turns the jet seemed to be on its course to Rota. "We'll be there soon, Audrey," Tom thought as he laid his head back and closed his eyes.

CHAPTER 18

Russell Stone awoke the next morning to a silence that he was not accustomed to since he had been on the Blue Star. He got up and slipped on his pants and shirt. He strapped on his shoulder holster and made his way to the bridge. Upon entering the bridge he found O'Brien and the ship's captain huddled together over a bank of instruments discussing something. As Stone entered O'Brien turned and looked at him.

"Good morning," O'Brien said.

"What's the problem?" Stone asked. "Why are we stopped?"

"Nothing serious," answered O'Brien. "We just had to shut down the engines for a while to replace a defective valve. We'll be back on the move in a few minutes. Just routine stuff, I didn't see any need to wake you."

"I appreciate that." Stone said. "But I don't mind if you wake me."

"O.K., I will next time." O'Brien said. Stone stepped over to the window and looked out onto the ocean. With the ship not making any headway, the Blue Star sat silently in the water. The ocean was calm and there was a light breeze. Stone checked his watch. It was seven thirty Greenwich time. In twenty-four hours they were scheduled to be docking at Port Said.

"Will we still make our schedule?" Stone asked.

"Yea, we will only lose thirty minutes or so," answered O'Brien. "We'll pick it up a few knots to make up for the delay." O'Brien checked his watch. "We'll dock in Said between eight and nine in the morning."

"Do you want a cup of coffee?" Stone asked.

"Sure would." O'Brien answered enthusiastically.

"Be back in a few minutes." Stone said as he left the wheelhouse and headed for the galley. Stone could smell the food being cooked as soon as he left the wheelhouse. Everyone else must still be in their bunks or on guard duty because the only other person in the galley was the cook. The cook saw Stone enter and smiled and pointed at the fresh biscuits on the counter. Stone put two cups of coffee, a couple of biscuits and some packets of jam on a tray and carried them back up to the wheelhouse. Just as Stone entered the wheelhouse he felt a rumble from deep in the bowels of the big boat. He looked at O'Brien who gave him the thumbs up.

"Engines back online," he said. "We'll be underway in a few minutes."

"Excellent." Stone replied as he set the tray down on the chart table. "The cook has groceries ready down stairs. This ought to hold you until you get down there."

"Thanks, man." O'Brien said as he picked up one of the coffees. Stone put some jelly on one of the biscuits and took a bite. He sipped his coffee and watched as the captain picked up the ship phone. He called down to the engine room and gave a series of instructions to the engineer. Soon Stone felt the big ship begin to move. Slowly the big freighter began to make headway. Stone watched as the bow slowly created a wake, which grew larger over the next few minutes.

Stone's attention turned to O'Brien when his PCU crackled. The SEAL making the call said that the two of them should come to the cells where the original crew was being held.

"On our way," answered O'Brien. They set down the coffee cups and made their way two decks lower to the cells. Entering the companionway containing the cells they saw the team member standing guard.

"What's up?" O'Brien asked. The guard, Petty Officer Jorge Mendoza had been having a conversation with one of the Spanish crewmen and he was able to learn a little about the future plans for the kidnapped girls.

"Sir, talking to the guy in the cell back there." Mendoza pointed back down the companionway. "The guy said he over-heard the captain talking on the radio before they sailed from the Bahamas. He said he heard him talking about unloading the "special cargo" at Port Said."

"Good." O'Brien said. "The captain didn't lie to me. That is what he told us during our debriefing." He glanced at Stone. "That helps. We can go ahead and let the command post know that Port Said has been confirmed. Good work Mendoza. Make sure you get relief so you can get some hot food. I understand the cook is rock'n and roll'n."

"Thank you, sir. I will." Mendoza said.

* * * * * * *

It was a sunny morning in the southwest of Spain on the Atlantic shore. The sky was a deep blue and the air cool. Audrey Clark stood outside the operations building next to the runway at Rota. She was holding Janet's hand and wearing a new pair of jeans, a light blue cotton shirt and a new pair of tennis shoes. After buying the new clothes, Janet took her to the hair stylist and got her hair trimmed and styled the way she liked to wear it. Audrey was excited about finally getting to see her parents.

"Which way will the airplane come from?" she asked Janet, looking back and forth at the opposite ends of the runway.

"I don't know." Janet answered. "But the airplane will look like one of those over there," she said pointing at a couple of small grey transport jets parked on the tarmac beside the operations hanger. Audrey looked over at the jets.

"O.K.," she said. "Those are much smaller than the ones that my dad usually flies on in Atlanta."

"Yeah, the Navy uses these jets to fly small numbers of people around." Janet said. "Those jets will only seat eight people, ten including the pilots." Suddenly Audrey pointed to the eastern end of the runway. "Look," she said. Janet turned and saw a small grey jet descending toward the end of the runway. Audrey and Janet watched as the wheels smoked when the jet touched down and rolled past them toward the other end. The jet rolled nearly to a stop and then turned and entered the taxi way and headed toward the two girls. Janet could feel Audrey's grip on her hand tighten as the jet approached.

"Is that my mom and dad?" Audrey asked excitedly.

"I think it might be." Janet answered. The guys in operations told her the flight with the Clarks was the only one due in that morning. The jet eventually made its way to the unloading area in front of the operations building. Audrey tried to move closer to the jet but Janet told her that they had to stand there until the steps were down and the passengers disembarked. Audrey fidgeted nervously until she saw the door open and the steps being lowered. After a few moments a girl in a Navy uniform exited and stood beside the steps. Janet began to let Audrey move a little closer. Soon another figure appeared in the doorway.

"Mommy!" Audrey yelled and broke loose from Janet and ran toward the jet. Janet followed along behind. Rachel Clark heard her daughter and hurried down the steps. Tom Clark followed his wife out of the aircraft and onto the tarmac. He had not seen Audrey yet and wondered why Rachel had taken off at a trot. He finally noticed Audrey running toward them. Rachel reached out and grabbed her daughter. She fell to her knees and they wrapped their arms around each other. Tom caught up to his wife and daughter and knelt beside them. He put his arms around them both as Rachel began to cry.

* * * * * * *

The morning after the tearful reunion on the tarmac in Spain, the Blue Star docked at Port Said. The captain and crew turned out to be very cooperative in preparing the ship for docking and in describing what will be done once they have docked. The SEAL platoon was well trained in convincing people that it was definitely in the crews interest to cooperate with them. The captain and crew understood that if they did as they were told and behave normally during their activities, they would be allowed to continue on their way once the SEALs mission was complete. Two SEAL members would remain on board the Blue Star to control and monitor the ship. They would be retrieved once the mission was over.

The captain made his normal contacts to arrange for the unloading of the Blue Star. As it turned out, the unloading of the legitimate cargo would be delayed until the dock personnel were available, most likely later in the day, probably late after noon. The men who were to pick up the "special" cargo knew only what day the ship was to arrive. The captain was required to notify them on actual arrival. The captain made the second call and was informed that the transfer of the prisoners would take place tonight after dark. In the meantime the SEAL platoon would go ashore and make contact with the advance team. A truck had been procured for the SEAL's use.

With a little time to kill the SEALs took care of last minute details. They made certain that their clothing was authentic, they cleaned and checked their weapons and ate a final meal aboard the ship. The cook had done an excellent job and the SEAL platoon showed their appreciation by leaving him a generous tip. They hoped he would be able to convert U.S. Dollars into his native currency.

By mid-afternoon the SEAL platoon, less the two men who were remaining behind to monitor the Blue Star, were in the truck and prepared to tail the prisoners. The vehicle was parked beside a warehouse and it was facing the freighter. Stone and O'Brien watched as the warehouse crews approached the ship and began to unload her. Nightfall was still a couple of hours away so the team would have to sit and wait for a while. The guys in the back of the truck decided to pass the time by playing cards. The docks at Port Said were busy loading and unloading ships of every shape and size. The presence of the SEAL team in their truck did not seem to cause any concern among any of the people who passed by. They appeared to be waiting to receive a small shipment from one of the ships docked at the port.

It would take all night and into the morning to unload the grain and other material from the freighter but the crews would stop work and go home around nine PM. Stone and O'Brien assumed that the pick up of the prisoners would take place sometime after the dockworkers knocked off for the night. The captain of the Blue Star said that he would receive a telephone call about an hour before the pick up was made. O'Brien would receive a notification from the two SEALs aboard the ship when that call was received. Stone and the SEAL team would sit and wait until the vehicle arrived. Once it arrived, the vehicle would be tagged with an electronic bug that would allow it to be tracked by satellite. The tail vehicle would not have to maintain visual contact as the suspect vehicle would be monitored aboard the Anzio and on the portable GPS tracking device carried by O'Brien. The team was on the ground because other forms of insertion of the team would be more risky. O'Brien and his men would quietly follow the undercover prisoners until they reached their final destination, At which time the suspects would be apprehended and other possible victims would be rescued.

✳ ✳ ✳ ✳ ✳ ✳ ✳

The sun began to set over the Mediterranean. A few warehouses on the west side of the port hampered the view of the sunset from the truck. The view of the sea was blocked, but the colors exploding above the horizon were visible and were viewed with its due appreciation by Stone and O'Brien. Hopefully there would be only a few more hours of waiting before the dock workers knocked off for the evening. Stone was bored. The passenger seat of the truck was getting harder every minute. But as the thought crossed his mind, he remembered that the rest of the team was in the back of the truck and they were sitting on the floor or on the wooden benches along the sides. He was silently ashamed of himself.

"Shouldn't be much longer." Stone said trying to remain positive about the sitting and waiting.

"Hopefully it will only be a couple of more hours." O'Brien acknowledged as he stretched his legs as much as he could inside the truck. He shifted his position in the seat and then continued to study the detailed map of Port Said and its vicinity. The two men settled back into their waiting mode when O'Brien's PCU crackled.

"O'Brien here, go ahead," he said into the mouthpiece. He listened for a few seconds and then nodded his head. "Understood, out." O'Brien looked over at Stone. "The call was received. They are preparing the captives for transfer."

"Alright." Stone said. "Here we go." O'Brien turned and looked through the hole in the rear of the cab and informed the rest of the team that the call had been received and they should be on their way soon. A joint sigh of relief was heard emanating from the rear of the truck along with more than enough sarcasm peppered with four-letter words. O'Brien smiled. At least the phone call broke up the monotony.

"Your team is well trained and dedicated." Stone said. "The victims of these bastards are lucky to have such a team looking out for them."

"Thanks, on behalf of the team." O'Brien said. "These guys do work hard, I'm honored to command such a tough and dedicated group of guys." Stone acknowledged with a nod and both men sat silent for a few minutes.

"I hope the hostages are transported by truck to the final destination." Stone said more to himself than to O'Brien.

"Yeah, I don't want to have to risk flying through all of this unpredictable airspace." O'Brien said considering their backup transportation was a small jet sitting on a small runway outside of Port Said. "Flying around attracts a lot more attention than driving does."

"Look." Stone said. He was pointing toward the Blue Star. A medium size Mercedes cargo truck pulled up and parked in front of the freighter. A few seconds later two men got out and went on board the ship. Stone and O'Brien watched as a man slipped out of the darkness from under the walkway to the ship and rolled under the Mercedes truck. A few seconds later the figure rolled out from under the truck and disappeared again under the walkway.

"The bug is in place." O'Brien said. He reached into his bag and retrieved a small black piece of electronic equipment. He turned it on and pressed a series of commands and a small character lit up on the LCD screen indicating the trucks position on a map of Port Said. The entire Mediterranean area and the Middle East were stored in the handheld GPS unit in O'Brien's hand.

* * * * * * *

Stone and O'Brien continued to observe the activities and watched as the six "hostages" were taken off the ship and placed in the back of the truck. Stone noticed that the "hostages'" hands were tied behind their backs and it appeared from Stones view point that they were also gagged but there were no hoods over there heads. Stone assumed that once they were on the truck the hoods would be replaced. The captain of the Blue Star and the driver of the truck stood on the dock and spoke to each other for a few seconds. Then the driver reached into the cab of the truck. He retrieved a small brown bag and handed it to the captain. The captain accepted the bag and returned to the ship.

"Payment for services rendered, I guess." O'Brien said. Then he turned and told the team that they would be on their way soon. Stone and O'Brien watched as the driver got into the cab of the truck and the second man climbed into the back with the "hostages." The cargo truck started its engine and turned around. O'Brien started his truck. He waited for a few seconds and then pulled out and fell in behind the cargo truck keeping a safe distance as Stone monitored the vehicles progress on the streets of Port Said. After leaving the city streets, Stone and the SEAL team followed the Mercedes west along a road across the desert in the direction of Israel and Jordan.

The trucks drove west stopping only for gas and finally reached the outskirts of Amman, Jordan. The trip across Israel had been uneventful, stopping only twice at check points. The SEAL's papers and their disguises worked as expected. The truck was examined briefly and then allowed to pass. Stone and O'Brien wondered if this was their destination when the driver pulled over at a small restaurant. The other man stayed in the truck. A few minutes later the driver came out of the restaurant and handed something to the man in the back. The driver got back into the cab with a small brown bag of his own. Stone assumed they just stopped to get food. The cargo truck started its engine again and pulled back onto the highway. The SEALs followed the truck through Amman and out the north side. Stone checked his map.

"Next stop, Damascus." Stone said. He was silently hoping that they didn't have to follow these guys much further. "Syria would be a logical location for the home of such an operation. The history of Syria's international behavior is studded with terrorist activities."

"I have a feeling that is where we are headed." O'Brien said. "We are going to have to be extremely careful. The U.S. doesn't have many friends in Syria." The SEALs followed well behind the Mercedes, well out of sight, for the next five hours.

CHAPTER 19

Shortly before sunrise, about fifteen hours after leaving the dock in Port Said, Stone and the SEALs followed the cargo truck with the undercover operatives to the northwestern side of Damascus. The cargo truck eventually pulled up to the gate at a guarded compound. O'Brien surveyed the terrain and noticed some high ground to the west of the compound where he should be able to hide the truck and observe the activities at the compound. O'Brien was able to find a small place to park the truck off the road behind a small hill and some bushes. He dispatched two of the team members from the rear of the truck to scout the area and watch the compound. The two men dismounted and ran to the crest of the hill undercover of the trees and settled in to monitor their objective. The remaining SEALs along with Stone and O'Brien removed their gear and weapons from the hidden compartments in the trucks body. All gear was inspected and accounted for. Each team member took the weapon, explosive or equipment that was assigned to him. Each man donned his Personal Communications Unit (PCU) and they did a communications check.

The men that left earlier to monitor the compound did not yet have their comm gear so O'Brien headed up the little hill to deliver theirs. Once he got to the observers position he was informed that the hostages were taken from the truck and placed inside a small block building just inside the gate. The two men in the truck were met by another man who opened the small building and helped move the hostages into it. Otherwise, there had been no other movement within the compound.

After securing the hostages, the driver parked the truck beside the main building and they all went inside.

Stone joined O'Brien and the other two on the hill. They surveyed the compound and its perimeter. Surrounding the entire compound was a small wall topped with barbed wire. There were four small guardhouses, one at each corner of the wall. Mounted on a pole just inside the wall were lights pointing out from the facility but they were not on. Each guardhouse had one guard inside but they did not seem to be too worried about any kind of attack. The defenses appeared to be just a precaution against someone just wondering onto the grounds. O'Brien also noticed cameras mounted on the side of the building, they were not rotating and he could not see any evidence that they were actually operational, but he had to assume that they were. O'Brien decided that there was no reason to delay. Stone and O'Brien returned to the truck. O'Brien retrieved his satellite communications device from his gear. He entered a code into it that would inform all of their support units that the operation was a go and was commencing within the hour.

* * * * * * *

The Anzio and the other ships in the Mediterranean had monitored the movements of both trucks since the outset of the operation. When the go signal was received a message was sent to two Blackhawk helicopters that had been monitoring the movements of the SEALs from within U.S. occupied Iraq. The Blackhawks lifted off from the desert floor inside Iraq and proceeded just above ground level to the compound outside of Damascus. The two Blackhawks were equipped with state of the art electronic gear that rendered them virtually invisible to most air defense systems in the world. As long as the two aircraft remained out of visual detection by Syrian air defenses, they should be able to complete their mission with total anonymity.

* * * * * * *

Lt. O'Brien and Russell Stone lay atop the little hill, under the small trees and watched as the SEAL team members stealthily made their way to their assigned staging areas. The lights inside the compound still had not come on. If there were motion detectors installed around the perimeter, they would probably activate the lights if movement was detected. So far the SEALs had been able to move without activating the lights. Soon there was no movement observed by O'Brien or Stone. The SEALs were in position. Stone observed through his binoculars as each guardhouse was neutralized and occupied by a SEAL team member. They did find television monitors in each guardhouse but they were not operating. A fifth and sixth team member approached the main gate and opened it after a thorough inspection for detection devices, which were found and bypassed. Stone and O'Brien left the cover of the trees and made their way to the opened gate. When they arrived at the gate the small block building door was already opened and the undercover hostages were released. Once the bonds were removed the women rubbed the sore areas of their arms where the ropes had bound them. The six heroic women immediately assumed their tactical roles for the remainder of the operation, accepting the weapons and gear handed them by O'Brien and Stone. Two team members proceeded to search the exterior of the compound as the rest of the assault team made their way to the entrances of the building.

* * * * * * *

The assault teams entered the residence quickly and quietly, surprised that there was no resistance. Stone followed one group into the building and O'Brien followed another. The teams cleared the interior and identified the individual rooms. Stone followed two team members down a hallway until they stood outside what appeared to be a large room with a big ornate door. The door was not locked and the three men opened the door and quietly entered a large well decorated den area. There was a fireplace but there was not a fire. The walls were decorated with pictures along with memorabilia typical of a wealthy person. Stone noticed a door to the right of the fireplace, which was ornate like the other one but not as large. Stone stepped to the door and tried the doorknob, it was unlocked. Stone opened it and peered into the room. He immediately noticed a large bed in the middle of the far wall and what appeared to be two people in it asleep. He motioned to the other two team members that he had found two people. They joined him at the door and the three entered the room and made their way to the sides of the bed. The two SEAL's held their weapons with the sights at their eyes with one hand and reached over to the sleeping people simultaneously. Stone switched on the light in the room as a strong hand placed over their mouths abruptly awakened the sleeping people.

O'Brien and the other team members managed to wake up four other guards inside the residence and subdue them. Each room was cleared as they were found. O'Brien made his way down a short hallway that appeared to lead toward the kitchen area. He stopped at a door on the right wall and slowly opened it. The door had been locked from the outside. O'Brien eased it open and saw that there was a small platform, which ended with stairs going down into what smelled like a laundry room. O'Brien motioned for the other two SEAL's to continue clearing the building. He slowly entered the stairwell and finding a light switch, he flipped it on. The stairs became illuminated and he carefully went down the steps. He had been correct. There were several washing machines along one wall and a couple of dryers. The room was neat and clean. He turned toward a white door along the left wall and moved toward it. He turned the handle and slowly opened it. The room was dark but he could make out what appeared to be a bed on the back wall of the room. There was a form in the bed. He held his weapon up to his eyes and reached for the light switch. As soon as he flipped the switch he glanced quickly around the room and then concentrated on the form in the bed.

Michele woke when the light came on. She was accustomed to Sima waking her up at odd hours to wash laundry or perform some other chore. But this time when she opened her eyes she was staring into the barrel of a gun. She was about to scream when she saw the man behind the gun lower it and hold his finger up to his lips indicating that she should be quiet. Michele felt reassured that the man did not mean her any harm. She was not sure, she just trusted him.

"Do you speak English?" O'Brien asked quietly. Michele struggled to answer but she was overcome by conflicting emotions. She was scared and did not really know if the man meant to hurt her or not. But she also recognized a purely American voice.

"Yes, Yes." Michele finally said. "I am from New York. Are....are you here to take me home?" O'Brien suddenly realized that this girl was someone they'd hoped they would find and be able to rescue. He was suddenly having trouble controlling his emotions. He looked at her imagining what she must have gone through. She was just a young girl that had been stolen from her family and forced into slavery. He looked at her and tried to smile reassuringly.

"Yes, we'll take you home. What is your name?" he asked missing it when she said it before.

My name is Mish....Michele." she said with a little smile. O'Brien smiled back and crouched down beside the bed and took her hand.

"Michelle, my name is O'Brien. How long have you been here?" He asked with a feeling of accomplishment and pride growing inside. Any doubts he may have had about the worthiness of this mission were now erased. The girl hesitated as if she were deep in thought.

"I...I don't know," she said feeling confused. "I've been here a long time, though." O'Brien felt sorry for the little girl. He put his hand on her shoulder.

"Well, we will get you home, O.K., but my men and I still have some work to do before we can leave." He told her. "I need you to get your clothes on and come with me. And I need you to be real quiet and do exactly what we tell you, O.K." Michele smiled broadly at O'Brien.

"I can do that," she said as she jumped up out of bed and started looking for the clothes she wanted to wear home. She was happier than she had been in a very long time. Sima had taken away the clothes she was wearing when she arrived so she was forced to wear the Arab style clothes she was given. Michele could not believe that she was being rescued. She was excited, happy. She was going home. She missed her mother and father very badly. She looked over at the man who woke her. Who was this man? she asked herself. How did he know that she was here? She did not know the answers to the questions she was asking herself. She finally accepted the fact that he was going to take her home and she was happy about it.

O'Brien moved over to the door when she got up and he listened for activity in the rest of the building. No shot had been fired so far. All guards had been surprised and subdued. No one had really been hurt yet with the exception of the uncomfortable plastic bands used to tie hands and feet. Michele joined O'Brien at the door after she changed.

"I'm ready," she said excitedly.

"O.K." O'Brien answered. "Stay close to me and be very quiet." They moved out of her room and toward the stairs. After climbing the stairs they followed the hallway back to the large den. SEAL team members had found two more American girls in various parts of the compound and brought them to the den also. They were sitting on one of the leather sofas. One female undercover operative was with them. O'Brien took Michele to the sofa and introduced her to the others and told her to wait there with them. At that moment O'Brien's PCU crackled as one of the search teams contacted him.

"This is O'Brien," he said. "Go ahead."

"Sir, you might want to check out what we've found in the large building about one hundred meters east of the residence, over."

"Roger," replied O'Brien. "I'm on my way," he turned and looked at Michele.

"You stay here, Michele, we will be leaving soon," he said.

"O.K." Michele said. The female FBI agent stepped over to Michele and knelt down in front of her.

"Hello, Michele, my name is Karen," she said. "I'll be here with you guys until we leave, O.K. If you need anything let me know."

"Thank you." Michele said. O'Brien knew he was leaving Michele in good hands. So he went to the door to go see what his men had found in the other building.

* * * * * * *

Russell Stone held his weapon up to his eyes as he slowly pulled the sheets off of the two people that had just been abruptly awaken in the very well appointed bedroom. Stone recognized that one was an older man around sixty years old, obviously of Arab descent. The other was a girl who appeared to be about fifteen or sixteen, neither had any clothes on. Stone looked at the girl and asked her if she spoke English. The girl reached down and pulled the sheet back over her. She appeared confused and then seemed to comprehend Stone's question.

"Yea...Yes...I...I'm from San Diego," she struggled to say.

"Were you kidnapped?" Stone asked. The man in the bed finally realized that he was not dreaming. He started to get up but the SEAL on his side of the bed stopped him.

"Don't move!" the SEAL said loudly. The man froze for a second then looked over at Stone assuming he was in charge.

"What is this? Who the hell are you?" the man said in broken English. Stone looked from the girl to the man.

"Shut up." Stone said, staring hard into the man's eyes. "I will deal with you in a moment." The man moved as if to begin to say something. The SEAL swung the butt of his weapon and struck the man on the side of the face. The girl jumped with fear at the suddenness of the attack.

"It will be O.K." Stone said to the girl and she looked back at him. "Take the sheet and go get your clothes on." He held out his hand and helped her off the foot of the bed. "Do you want to return to San Diego?" he asked her. The girl stopped and stared at Stone, holding the sheet around her body. He could see tears forming in her eyes. She seemed to be trying to comprehend what was going on around her. She finally looked up at Stone.

"It has been so long," she said trying to hold back tears. "I think I've been here with these bastards for over two years," she said finally unable to control her emotions. She began to cry. Stone put his hand on her shoulder and looked into her eyes.

"What is your name?" the girl struggled with her tears and looked at Stone.

"My name is Sharon….Sharon Belk," she finally said. Stone nodded his head.

"O.K. Sharon we're here to take you home. Get your clothes on and we'll get you out of here." She nodded her head and walked toward the bathroom. She glanced back at the man in the bed, who appeared to be unconscious. Sharon pulled the sheet up tighter around her and moved quickly into the bathroom. Stone walked around to the right side of the bed and reached for the man lying there with a fresh gash on his face. Shaking him awake, Stone told him to get up. Slowly the man came to and shook his head. The man stood as he felt his face.

"You will pay for….." the man began, but Stones right fist interrupted his sentence. The man fell across the bed.

"Restrain him." Stone told the SEALs. The two men strapped his hands behind his back and strapped his feet together. "Pull him off onto the floor." Stone said to the SEALs. "Let him finish his nap on the cold, hard floor." Stone watched with pleasure as the SEALs drug the naked man off the bed with a thump and then out onto the tiled floor leaving a trail of blood. They let him lie on the floor with his hands and legs bound. One of the SEAL's took a small camera out of his pocket and took a couple of pictures of the old man lying on the floor. Soon Sharon came out of the bathroom and looked down at the man on the floor.

"Thank you," she said to the men standing beside him. "He deserves whatever you do to him." She walked over to Stone.

"My name is Russell Stone," he said to her. "Come on, let's get you to a safe place." Stone led her out into the den where he saw the other girls seated on the sofa. He took her over to Karen.

"Karen, this is Sharon," he said. "We need to get her back to her family in San Diego. O.K." Karen looked at Sharon and smiled.

"Hello Sharon. Let's wait here and as soon as we are finished we will be on our way." She led Sharon over to where the other girls were huddled together on the sofa. The girls had never seen each other before. They all introduced themselves and talked excitedly about finally being able to go home.

* * * * * * *

O'Brien walked the one hundred meters across the desert ground between the buildings and met the other SEAL Member outside of the large warehouse.

"I don't believe this is official stuff." The SEAL said. O'Brien followed him through the doorway. Three Arabs sat along the wall with their hands and feet bound and gags tied around their mouths. O'Brien followed the team member through another door and was pointed toward stacks of what obviously were weapons. As far as he could see were stacks of various size boxes, boxes that O'Brien was familiar with. There was enough military gear here to equip a small army. The SEALs had broken open a few of the crates to reveal a sample of the items in the warehouse. There were crates and crates of RPG's shoulder launched anti-aircraft weapons and AK-47's among other military hardware. The military equipment was reflective of the relationship between Syria and the old Soviet Union. Since the breakup of the communist state its military industrial complex was forced to continue marketing its wares to old established customers. Syria had been a long time client state of the failed empire. The majority of these arms were destined for the many enemies of Israel and the U.S. as well as any other entity that could afford the price.

"There is no need to leave this stuff lying around." O'Brien said. "Set charges with a remote, we'll blow it as we are leaving."

"There is enough plastic explosive in here to reduce this stuff to a pile of burning dust," the SEAL operative said. O'Brien looked in the direction of the tied up guards.

"Bring them back to the main building when you leave here. We'll put them all in a safe place so their countrymen can release them after we're gone." The SEAL's went to work wiring the explosives. O'Brien walked back to the main residence. All of the rooms had been cleared. All of the suspects were restrained and guarded. O'Brien activated his PCU and directed that all prisoners were to be brought into the den of the main residence. Once O'Brien's team and the victims had departed local officials would be notified and they would be responsible for the facility and personnel. O'Brien met Stone as he entered the residence.

"The mission appears to be a success." O'Brien said looking over at the young girls on the sofa.

"I believe you're right." Stone said with a smile. "Did you see the character in the bedroom?"

"No, not yet." O'Brien said. "Is he the ringleader?"

"Not sure." Stone said thoughtfully. "I think we need to transport him and all of the info we can gather and analyze it elsewhere and see where it leads us."

"Sounds good. I'll get a couple of men on it." O'Brien said. He looked to three of his team standing in the den and told them to search the building for any computers, file cabinets and anything else that may contain information concerning the business or other activities associated with this place and bring it all to the main entrance. The men hurried off to carry out O'Brien's orders.

Soon the den began to fill up with bound and gagged men and a few women as the SEALs carried out the orders given to them earlier. When Sima was brought into the room Michele looked at her. Michele felt sorry for her when she noticed the gag tied around her mouth and her hands tied behind her back. Michele got up from the sofa and walked over to O'Brien.

"O'Brien, could you please make her more comfortable?" Michele asked. "She was very nice to me. I feel sorry for her." O'Brien looked over at the woman Michele was talking about, and then he looked at Stone.

"If she trusts her, then so do I." Stone said.

"Come with me, Michele." He took her hand and they walked over to Sima who was sitting on the floor against the wall. O'Brien motioned for her to stand. She stood in front of him and he removed the gag from her mouth.

"Thank you," she said in awkward English. O'Brien motioned for her to turn around. She did and he cut the plastic strap that bound her hands. She turned back toward him.

"You may leave," he said. Sima smiled. She looked at Michele. The two had been placed in positions that neither one liked. Sima was sorry about what had happened to Michele and Michele knew how Sima felt. Sima had grown to love Michele. She admired Michele's strength. She was glad that Michele would be going home where she belonged. Sima was also sorry that she had come to work for a man like Rahish. Sima's life would be different from now on. She looked at Michele and put her hands on her shoulders.

"Goodbye, Misha," she said.

"Goodbye, Sima. Michele said and then she hugged Sima. They hugged for a few moments while the others in the room watched. Soon Michele pushed away and looked at Sima.

"You must leave now, Sima." Sima nodded her head. She turned and bowed her head slightly at O'Brien and thanked him. She made her way to the door and walked outside. Stone watched her as she walked up the driveway and out onto the little road that would take her to the little town a few miles away. Michele had followed her to the door and watched as she walked away.

"That was a very good thing to do," Stone said to Michele.

"She was good to me." Michele said. "I wish I could do more for her."

"I think you did more for her than you know." Stone said.

"I hope so." Michele said as Stone began to hear a deep thumping sound. Stone looked over at O'Brien.

"Helicopters." Stone said as O'Brien began to finger his PCU. Soon O'Brien was hailing the helicopters on the frequency that was assigned to the transport units. O'Brien made his way to the door and then outside the building. He and Stone looked toward the southeast and eventually the two Blackhawks came into view. The aircraft slowed as they found the compound and then landed just outside of the main entrance to the residence. O'Brien closed the door while the choppers landed to keep from being covered with sand.

* * * * * * *

As soon as they landed and opened the doors, O'Brien directed the kidnapped girls onto the first Blackhawk along with the female under-cover operatives. The second Blackhawk was loaded with the SEAL pla-toon, Stone, the captured computers and files and finally one naked sixty year old man. The remaining captives were left in the main room of the residence. Local authorities would release them once they were notified. After the Blackhawks were loaded and all gear and personnel were secure they lifted off and headed in a northwesterly direction. Stone watched as the buildings they had just left began to shrink in the distance. When the two birds were at a safe distance, the demolition expert on the SEAL team lifted the red safety guard on his control unit and pressed the but-ton. A split second later a huge explosion was heard by all of the pas-sengers aboard the helicopters. Since the explosion was to the rear of the Blackhawks no one could see it, but they could tell from the sound and the shock that it was sufficient to accomplish the task.

The Blackhawks set out on a course that would take them through a small amount of Syrian territory and then into Jordan on their way to an Israeli Defense Forces airfield outside of Tel Aviv. Personnel were there waiting to assist with any medical treatment that may be needed and also to collect the seized computers and files. The information would be analyzed for any additional information that may lead them to others involved in the kidnapping ring. The Israelis would also assume respon-sibility for the old man that was brought along. Hopefully his inter-rogation would reveal information that would be useful. They would certainly be interested in the warehouse full of weapons and it's target.

The Blackhawks were making excellent time toward the Jordanian border when O'Brien got a call from the pilot of the lead chopper in-forming him that they had been spotted by the Syrian air defense forces and that the passengers should prepare themselves for some rough flying. The pilots of the Blackhawks were receiving data from AWACS aircraft that were on station over Iraq and another AWACS that was on station over Israel. There were indications that Syrian MIGs were preparing to take off to intercept the American helicopters. Syrian anti-aircraft radars had also activated and were targeting the Blackhawks. O'Brien switched frequencies to his tactical channel and informed his team of the problem and for them to make preparations for a possible air battle. The sky over Syria was clear. Any attacking aircraft would probably be able to shoot down the Blackhawks by visual means. "Sure wish there was no moon this morning." O'Brien thought. But it was more important to get out of hostile airspace as quickly as possible. Waiting sixteen hours for the sun to go down would have been more risky than an immediate extraction, especially with the excellent electronic systems installed on the Blackhawks. They would not have been seen at all except for a tactical air defense unit that had been out on an exercise and had turned on its acquisition radar just as the Blackhawks flew over their position. The AWACS controllers had seen everything as it happened. They were now sending the Blackhawk pilots updated waypoint coordinates that should help them bypass or avoid the dangers ahead. Meanwhile, the MIG's did make their take off and turned on an intercept course with the Blackhawks. The chopper pilots dropped as close to the deck as they could safely fly and increased speed in an attempt to get out of danger before the MIG's could acquire them. The calculations received by the chopper pilots from the AWACS indicated the MIG's would intercept them about twenty kilometers short of the Jordanian border. But the Syrian pilots would not be very concerned about violating Jordanian airspace. Syria was the Arab power in the area and if Jordan complained Syria would just say their pilots were unaware of their position and the violation would be swept under the rug.

The two Blackhawks were flying low and fast when the MIG's finally appeared on their radars. The pilots knew that they were sitting ducks with the fast movers tracking them and they fully expected to be blown to bits within a few minutes. As the Syrian MIGs approached, the Blackhawk pilots radioed AWACS for help in avoiding the approaching MIGs.

The AWACS were strangely silent as the helicopters radars showed the enemy aircraft closing within weapons range of the helicopters. Russell Stone could sense the tension in the cockpit of the lead helicopter since he was sitting just to the rear of the co-pilot. He also was blessed with a lot of airtime in Blackhawks during his time in the Special Forces. He was actually qualified to fly these birds if necessary.

The noise inside the Blackhawk was too high to hear the pilot's conversation but he could tell by their activities and the readings on the gauges that there was danger. He turned so he could see out of the windscreen. The sky was blue and clear. Suddenly the co-pilot pointed at the radar screen and then out toward the front right of the helicopter. Stone was certain that their time had come. Stone tried to look but couldn't see in the direction the co-pilot had indicated. The pilot seemed to bear down on the controls as if to get as much distance out of his machine as he could before he went down. Stone recognized the heroism of the two men in the front of the chopper. If he was to go down, he knew that these men would have done their best to save the lives of those in their care.

The lead helicopter suddenly changed course. The quick turn to the left had caught all passengers off guard. The hard bank to the left seemed too abrupt and controlled to be accidental. Stone assumed the pilot was avoiding an air-to-air missile. Stone changed his gaze to the right side of the aircraft in time to see two explosions off in the distance, two or three thousand feet above and a couple of kilometers east of their position. The Blackhawks then made a turn back to the right and resumed more normal flight characteristics. Stone looked at O'Brien who was wiping the sweat from his brow and shrugging his shoulders. The pilot eventually turned and looked at Stone.

"Our Israeli friends just relieved us of our two problems," he said. "We are in Jordanian airspace and should be landing at Tel Aviv in about forty-five minutes." The pilot grinned and turned back toward the front.

CHAPTER 20

The two Israeli F-16 Falcons escorted the Blackhawks to the airstrip. As soon as the rotary wing aircraft had landed safely the fighters returned to their own base. Personnel from the U.S. Navy and the U.S. Embassy in Israel were waiting when Stone and the SEALs touched down. The hostages were loaded into a van and were taken to the base hospital for medical exams. Once the rotors of the helicopters had stopped spinning the pilots exited the cockpits and began congratulating the SEALs. The SEALs would have to work off the adrenaline that remains in the system for a while after the completion of a mission like this. Even though there were no shots fired, the stress was still there. Soon another vehicle pulled up beside the helicopters and one elderly Arab man was removed from the helicopter and loaded onto the van along with the confiscated computers and paper files. These items were headed for the headquarters of the Israeli Intelligence Service- the Mossad. There the material would be analyzed for any information that could possibly identify others who were involved in smuggling human beings and selling them into slavery. Stone and Lt. O'Brien watched as the vehicle pulled off with its passenger and intelligence material.

"Well, hopefully they will be able to get good intel out of that guy," O'Brien said.

"I believe they will crack him," Stone surmised, "in more ways than one, let's hope."

"Yea, that's what he deserves." O'Brien said. "Well, what is in store for you now, Russ?"

"I guess I need to call El Al and see if they have any flights back to the United States." Stone said suddenly realizing that his job was done. "It has been a pleasure working with you guys." Stone said reaching for O'Brien's hand to shake it.

"If we can be of service to you in the future, you call us." O'Brien said, shaking Stone's hand. "This mission was extremely satisfying, thanks for letting us help." Stone clapped O'Brien on the back.

"You're welcome. I couldn't have picked a better group of people to help with this one." Stone walked over and shook the hands of the rest of the SEAL team and said his goodbyes. He was bone tired and needed rest. After speaking to everyone, he picked up his gear and made his way to the operations center to inquire into a room for the night. When Stone reached the door of the operations building he heard the engines of the Blackhawks starting. He turned and watched as the SEAL team loaded up and the choppers slowly lifted off the tarmac. They turned on a heading toward the Mediterranean.

* * * * * * *

Stone caught a ride in the operations duty vehicle over to the bachelor officer's quarters. He picked up his key from the front desk and then found his room. After a long, hot shower, he laid down on the bed for a little rest. His body was tired. He had not had a good eight hours of sleep since leaving the states a week earlier. It was still early afternoon and Russ told himself that he could only nap for an hour or so, then he would get up and call for a flight home.

Four hours later Russ Stone woke up. The clock said five pm. Russ sat up and rubbed his eyes. He picked up the English language phone book and turned to the airlines. He was able to get a flight to New York leaving at nine pm. He hung up the phone, found his wallet in his bag and removed his long distance calling card. He dialed the operator to help place his call to home. He laid back on the bed and listened to the phone ring.

"Hello." Stone heard on the other end.

"Hello, honey." Stone said into the phone as he closed his eyes and smiled.

* * * * * * *

While Russell Stone was winging his way across the Atlantic, the data processing intelligence analysts at the Mossad in Tel Aviv completed the extraction of the data on Rahish's computers. The main frame had pulled out several names and an analysis of the emails revealed physical locations of other suspects. A message was sent to the Paris offices of Interpol. Messages were also sent to FBI headquarters and the Justice Department in Washington D.C. Soon a team was assembled and the proper paperwork was completed. The following morning they would make an arrest.

* * * * * * *

Paul Rahhim was up early today. There was a lot to be done. He still believed that six packages had arrived in Damascus the previous day. And there were four packages enroute from the west coast of the U.S. to Hong Kong. After his normal breakfast he would return to his flat and see to the business of the day. He was dressed well as usual. He picked up his Rolex and placed it on his left wrist. He put his money clip full of Euros into his pocket. He looked at himself in the mirror and was pleased with what he saw. Picking up his keys he headed for the door. He left his flat and walked down stairs to the main level then out into the city toward his usual café. As he began to walk down the sidewalk the doors opened on a parked car and four men emerged. They approached Rahhim. He heard a noise behind him and he turned. The man behind him stood close while the other four surrounded the two men.

"I am Inspector Legrand of Interpol," the man said. "And you are…" The man looked down at the paper in his hand. "Azim Abdulah Rahhim, is that correct?" Rahhim looked at the man closely and cocked his head a little to the side.

"Yes, I am Paul Rahhim," he said to Legrand. "What can I do for you?"

"Mr. Rahhim, I am afraid that we require your presence at our headquarters." Legrand said trying to stay off the subject of Rahhim's arrest until they got to headquarters.

"I'm afraid I don't understand." Rahhim protested. "I will be gald to help you anyway I can, but I see no need to accompany you gentlemen anywhere."

"Sir, I assure you that this is a serious matter and you would be better served if you would voluntarily cooperate." Legrand persisted. He would not spend very much time talking to this man on the street. If Rahhim did not cooperate he would use force. "Would you please come with us, sir?" Rahhim assumed a defiant posture as if to say that he did not intend to go anywhere with Legrand.

"I have powerful connections....." Rahhim began. Legrand understanding where this was headed, glanced at the men behind Rahhim and instantly Rahhim was immobilized, hand cuffed and place in the back of the sedan parked at the side of the street. As Rahhim was being forced into the sedan, Legrand took several photos of the process.

*   *   *   *   *   *

A couple of days following the arrest of Paul Rahhim on the street in Paris, Russell Stone was in his office once again lifting weights. He was pushing one hundred and fifty pounds up for the tenth time when his wife walked in. She stood above his head while he strained at the bar. She looked down at him with her beautiful smile. He weakened.

"The mail is here you have a package," she said. Russ dropped the bar into the rack and sat up. He swung his leg over and sat sideways on the bench. His wife walked around to the side of the bench and handed him the package. Russ wiped his face with his towel and reached for it. She held on to it tightly making him have to pull on it hard. She finally let go and giggled.

"Playful today, are we," Russ said as he looked at the small parcel. He read the return address. It was from Paris. He carefully opened it and

182

pulled out the contents. There was a note and a couple of photographs. He read the note. It was short and to the point.

"We got the bad guy, Thought you might like to have these." He glanced at the pictures and smiled. Russ looked up at his wife. He tossed the photos and the note on the desk and reached for her. He pulled her onto his lap and kissed her.

"You're all sweaty," she said with a laugh. Russ held her as he rolled off onto the floor.

"That's alright. If you're lucky you will be too, soon." Then he kissed her again.

A few days later on a cool early fall day in Atlanta, Georgia, Tom Clark got out of his car in his driveway and walked over to the mailbox. He extracted the mail and looked through it. One piece caught his eye. It was hand addressed from the Washington D.C. area. He opened the letter as he heard the front door to his house open. He looked and saw his two daughters running out the door followed slowly by Rachel. He removed the contents from the envelope. Audrey and Mellisa finally got to him yelling, "Daddy, you're home." Tom looked at the note and the two photos. The note was short and to the point.

"Thought you might want to see these. Have a good day. RS" As his two beautiful daughters tugged on him to get him into the house, Tom looked at the pictures. One showed an old naked man lying on a floor with his hands and feet bound. The second picture was of a well dressed man struggling as four men push him into the back seat of a car. Tom smiled. Rachel finally reached him.

"What's in the mail today? Bills?" she asked. Tom smiled at her and hugged his girls.

"No," Tom said. "Actually payment... a little payment."

Breinigsville, PA USA
04 September 2009
223547BV00004B/2/P